Seven Wives:
A Romance

Books by Jonathan Baumbach

Seven Wives: A Romance
Separate Hours
The Life and Times of Major Fiction
My Father More or Less
The Return of Service
Chez Charlotte and Emily
Babble
Reruns
What Comes Next
A Man to Conjure With
The Landscape of Nightmare: Studies in the Contemporary American Novel

Seven Wives: A Romance

a novel by

Jonathan Baumbach

Boulder • Normal

First edition
First printing 1994

Published by Fiction Collective Two with support given by the English Department Publications Unit of Illinois State University, the English Department Publications Center of the University of Colorado at Boulder, the Illinois Arts Council, and the National Endowment for the Arts

Grateful acknowledgement is made to *Fiction International* and the anthology *Voices Louder Than Words* in which sections of this novel first appeared

Grateful acknowledgement is made to the Rockefeller Foundation for giving me the time and space to work on this novel at the Villa Serbelloni in Bellagio

Address all inquiries to: Fiction Collective Two, c/o English Department, Publications Center, College Box 494, University of Colorado at Boulder, Boulder, CO 80309-0494

Seven Wives: A Romance
Jonathan Baumbach

ISBN: Cloth, 0-932511-86-4, $18.95
ISBN: Paper, 0-932511-87-2, $8.95

Produced and printed in the United States of America
Distributed by The Talman Company

Cover/Jacket design: Dave LaFleur

To the women in my life:
Annette,
my daughter Nina,
my mother Ida,
former wives,
former loves

As I was going to Saint Ives
I met a man with seven wives.
Every wife had seven sacks,
Every sack had seven cats,
Every cat had seven kits,
Kits, cats, sacks and wives,
How many were going to Saint Ives?

—anonymous, As I Was Going to Saint Ives

0

The Narrator Presents Himself as a Suspicious Person

I have survived a series of unlikely attempts on my life. Someone out there—person or persons unknown—wants me erased. That's all I will say at this point without one of my former therapists in the room to validate my sanity. As to the presumptive assailant, I have several candidates in mind with unassailable credentials, more than a few theories, a steamer trunk full of suspicions. This is the way I went about my investigation: I wrote down on a legal pad all the people I had wronged (whose names I could still remember) and under that all the people who had wronged me (and who probably blamed me for their unspeakable behavior), a combined list that extended itself into the hundreds. I am an abrasive personality, though secretly soft-hearted. My second list, which was shorter, was comprised of acquaintances who imagined themselves wronged by me. These as a group were the least stable, the most likely to pursue vengeance years after the presumed offense. Then I accounted those for whom grievance was a way of life, people who couldn't cross the street without feeling disrespected by some passing car. Not to be omitted from consideration were former wives, all of whom fit into one or another of the categories. And then there were the women that I didn't marry, the ones who wanted (or said they wanted) greater intimacy, and the ones who wanted mostly to be left alone, and the ones who seemed to want both greater intimacy and to be left alone, women who thrived on the *frisson* of ambiguity.

Of course there is always the possibility of circumstantial enmity, displaced vindictiveness. Whenever possible, I try to stay clear of the incomprehensible. Down that road lies madness.

I occupy myself studying the emotional fingerprints of the failed attempts on my life in order that my list of potential enemies might narrow itself down to manageable anxiety. The first attempt was in the form of a glass of milk left at my bedtable one night. I could tell the milk was poisoned from its seductive whiteness as if a lit bulb were hidden inside the glass. This astonishingly white liquid was the dream of milk rather than the real thing. The presence of the milk was not surprising in itself. It was no secret that I was having trouble sleeping through the night. Everyone who knew me knew that; all of my wives and all of their confidantes knew my predilection for warm milk laced with brandy before bed. I poured the milk down the toilet at first opportunity, but told no one—not that there was anyone to tell. Except for the eerie glow of the milk and its corrosive effect on the enamel of the toilet, I had no conclusive proof that the milk was meant to do me harm.

If it was only the poisoned milk, I might have put its presence down to unacknowledged suicidal impulse and let the matter die. Subsequent attacks were harder to ignore. A nail the size of an icepick in the back tire of a rented car, tainted oysters, perfect-seeming apples with poisonous worms at their core, heart-piercing phone calls, a black widow spider hanging by a thread over my pillow, a sniper in the shadows of the roof across the way. A man of about my height and weight coming out of a restaurant in Chinatown on a Thursday night was beaten to death with a frozen duck. It was a restaurant I used to dine at regularly on Thursday nights a few years back.

A man with a similar last name was drowned to death in an inch of water in a model bathroom in a mobile homes exhibition in a town in Oregon, which had been the location for two scenes in a movie I had worked on not so long ago.

Someone wearing a raincoat like mine—a black Burberry with a torn belt loop—was pushed or fell of his own accord from a 14th story window of the Flatiron

Building in New York City.

It was all circumstantial evidence, a paranoid's wish list, nothing that didn't slip away with the shadows when the light went on.

The other attempts, perhaps they were warnings rather than attempts, were similarly oblique, inexplicable accidents in public places, bizarre coming attractions for the movie of my death.

When you look at the evidence as closely as I have, the inescapable conclusion is that there is more than one person involved. The evidence, as I read it, suggests there are at least four and possibly seven assailants working in concert or separately, with or without the direct knowledge of the others, or in casual uncoordinated collaboration. The obliqueness of the attempts suggest subtlety and patience, feminine malice, vengeance caked in ice.

Forget the above. This is my real theory, the distillation of my other theories, the conclusion to which all my other conclusions lead. I am the target of a conspiracy of women. My former wives are behind this invisible cabal, have banded together (with unknown others) out of common ideological ground and a passion for revenge, or for no reason at all. If you want women too much, want them in and out of your life, can't let go, can't hold on, you end up paying a disastrous price for it in the end. Women you no longer love never forgive you. Women who once loved you hold you responsible forever for their disappointment.

Wives. Wives, in my opinion, are never without homicidal motive, not even when asleep or in the act of love.

After seven marriages I have come to respect caution. When I hear a delicate knock at the door, something barely perceptible and deceptively gentle, I am not taken in. What I do, which is a long standing trick of mine, is pretend to be out. I sit absolutely still in a dark corner of the room, my mind elsewhere, my mind anywhere else. This is New York City after all. This is the future the anti-utopians warned us about. This is the apocalyptic future in the disguise of the benumbed present.

When the knock recurs after ten minutes of taunting silence, I am faced with a dilemma. Do I go for my gun which is in the back of a closet in another room, or do I remain motionless, pretend not to be at home? I've reached a point in my life where I'll do virtually anything to avoid commerce with the outside world. My worst dreams involve lethal intruders.

This is the basic scenario of my unconscious. I get a warning on the phone from an unidentifiable though familiar female voice. Someone wearing a fright mask, says my sly informant, has gotten into my penthouse apartment and is planning to kill me. The moment I hang up the phone, a large shadow moves from behind a curtain. A gun finds its way into my hand and is pointed at the space where the moving shadow has taken repose. I mean to say something, to call the apparent intruder to account, but I find I have no voice. A spasm in my finger causes the trigger to tilt, and the gun explodes like a tubercular cough. Someone or something falls. It is a bystander as it turns out, an innocent who somehow had gotten in the way. My apology is insufficient. A woman lies in a heap on the floor, dead or dying, irreparably harmed. I do what I can do, try to shake her from her sleep, breathe air into her lungs, but nothing avails. The police are at the door faster than might be expected, banging with their heavy fists. Out of panic, I offer the money under the mattress of my bed as restitution. Take half, I say, take all. My regret is sincere. Whatever I offer is not enough. Your crime is unforgivable, they say. You will know what real regret is when we get through with you.

I tend to wake from these dreams with a monumental hard-on. What's going on?

I slip off my shoes without bothering to untie the laces. In my stocking feet I am a ghostly presence as I move down the hall away from the barely perceptible knocking. It is my intention in all things not to give myself away.

The phone rings before I can reach the closet. I let it ring fifteen, twenty times, which should be enough to discourage even an assassin, before picking up the receiver. I say nothing. The voice inside the speaker rages against my palm.

The voice: "You are one hard person to reach. Don't you ever answer your phone?" The question is as familiar as the voice.

The voice presumes an intimacy, offers neither name nor information, only itself—its soft deep actressy seduction. I return the cordless phone to its bed.

The closet is permeated with the smell of mothballs or dry rot. The rows of woolen jackets seem to be deconvalescing on their hangers. At first the gun isn't at home, not where I remember giving it quarters. That worries me. But then I realize it is a matter of digging deeper—the gun wrapped in a Princeton sweatshirt in the deepest reaches of the high shelf. A large box trips off the shelf and I catch it, my legs buckling as I embrace its weight. It is a box of letters, mostly from women, assembled evidence, which I plan never to read again.

The immediate danger seems to have passed. The knocking at the door, which has stopped, is clearly not the real thing, just another form of inconsequential threat. When they're ready to take me out, there'll be no warning. I go into the kitchen and make myself a cup of tea. Even though it is scalding, even though it burns the lining of my throat, I slug it down, anticipating whatever unimaginable unpleasantness comes next.

Standing on a chair, I take down the orange sweatshirt, cradle its burden against my chest. As I unwrap the 30-caliber pistol, I calm myself by saying, "There isn't anything you can't handle, Jack." I note that the gun is loaded and that the safety is on.

I have a momentary failure of confidence, worry that the pistol won't fire (I have not used it, have not fired any kind of gun in years) or that my aim will be inaccurate. It sits in my lap like a pet. Then it takes its place on the seat next to me.

I know I have dozed on the couch, awake and asleep at the same time, because the doorbell startles me. Gun crawls into hand. I am on my feet. Door approaches. "Yes?" I say.

"I have to talk to you," a woman's voice says.

I hold the gun in front of me with both hands, aim at the door just above the knob. "It's the middle of the night, an inappropriate time. Come back tomorrow."

"It's important that I talk to you now," she says.

"About what, for God's sake. What's so important?

She laughs. "Nothing," she says. "Trust me. I wouldn't be here if it wasn't important."

Against all judgment, a victim of my own curiosity, I unlatch the door and step behind it. "It's open," I hear myself say.

For what seems like several minutes, there is not even a heartbeat on the other side of the door. It is a silence enhanced to an unbearable non-pitch.

A light fixture behind me flickers, and I turn my head for what seems like no time. When I turn back, the door is already open, and a largish woman is standing, moving slowly, just inside the plane of the room. The light behind my ear flickers twice more, then makes a popping sound.

Everything is shadows at this point, black on gray. The unrelieved dark is harbored in my eyes. The gun is out in front of me, pointed at the shadow that seems intent on coming at me. I promise myself not to fire prematurely.

I fire a warning shot—the gun goes off against my intention to assess the situation a moment longer. The art deco standing lamp with the glass shade goes over, sparks flying from the outlet as the cord tears itself from the wall. Damn! There is another crash,the second eating into the first as the woman stalking me also falls.

There is an afterimage apparently illuminated from the sparks coming out of the wall. I know, without actually seeing her, that the falling woman is my fifth wife, Cara Lou. When I get the light on, I discover her lying in a puddle of shattered glass.

I feel for her pulse, put my ear against her heart. There are distant murmurs like trapped voices. I can find no wound. If there is no wound, then why is there no pulse? My own breathing is so loud, it may have drowned hers out. I stand up, brush the diamonds of glass from my knees, and notice, looking idly now at the body, a circular mark on the temple, abutting the hairline. The longer I study the mark, which gives off a kind of glow, the more pronounced it seems. When I get closer I can see that it might be a wound—it stares like a tiny doll's eye—but I am almost sure it is too small to have been made by a bullet.

I sit slumped in a chair, the lamplight directly in my face as if I were the subject of a grilling in a detective movie. The room has been restored, the body removed.

I had lost some money in the market. It was a time when everyone except the inside insiders were suffering major losses. My habits had become too expensive for my present income. The first place I cut back was the alimony payments, which I hated to pay out anyway, which I never saw the sense in, which I had only agreed to because my lawyers said that was the way it was done.

Lawyers: a hateful profession in my experience. I never dealt with one who didn't somewhere along the way feed off human misery, usually mine. They exist to protect us from our better instincts whether we have them or not.

When the letters came from my wives' lawyers, I threw them away unopened or set them on fire in a metal wastebasket, burning the lawyers themselves in a kind of effigy.

It was about that time, the time of the threatening unopened letters, the time of the attempts on my life, the time of my bad dreams that were dreams within dreams (the usual emotional sewage), that I began to cut down on my excursions outside the apartment. There seemed less and less need to go out. I had my food and video tapes delivered. I used personal checks or plastic for all my purchases. There was no need, there was less and less need, to risk transaction with the unpredictable streets.

This too I discovered, that I was less lonely by myself in the midst of paraphernalia of day-to-day ordinary life than I was loose in the world, outside of my element, in the company of others.

Everything I did, mostly everything, was in the cause of safety. No, scratch that—not safety but survival, which has always been my primary goal. What I relied on, what comforted me, was that I knew that there was no one of my closest acquaintance (I'm talking about wives and lovers, family, apparent friends, people who worked for me, people I worked for) I could dare to trust. To trust no one is a state so pure it amounts to religious experience.

Have I learned anything from my experiences with

women? Yes, but what?

I wake this morning with a whole new plan for my life. I'm going to start this morning after breakfast—I postpone eating for as long as I can resist it—to write the story of my seven failed marriages, my life as domestic man, as a cautionary tale. "Do as I didn't" will be the thesis of my book. Avoid my mistakes or avoid my regrets. Also, I want to complete my life, to learn what I learned from it, before my life, as it will, completes me. I have been keeping a journal off and on since high school. Some of the volumes have been destroyed, some left behind without hope of recovery. I tend to be precipitous in my behavior, to flee even my own shadow when it begins to oppress me.

If I seem to hate my former wives (it is mostly the other way around—their animosity, not mine), it is because I loved them, love them still, keep them alive and kicking in memory.

Although I have a word processor and two electronic typewriters at my disposal, I decide to work in long hand (a more humanistic approach), using a felt-tip pen on a legal pad. I have a title (it came to me in a dream the night before): "Meeting A Man Who Had Seven Wives," which I write in capital letters at the top of the page. It is a start, the claiming of context.

In the next hour, I write several first sentences—actually, eight or nine, none precisely what the story requires. I settle on: "He had survived several unlikely attempts on his life." At the end of the day, in which I have written two surviving pages, I am ready to discard the project. Though accurate, it reads, much of it, like elaborate circumventions of the truth, disguised lies.

A phone call to a former agent who owes me a favor opens up a new possibility for my project. "Get a ghost, sweetheart," Olympia tells me. "No one who has had a life like yours writes his own autobiography in America in 1992."

She offers to put me in touch with one of her favorite clients, an avant-garde novelist who sometimes writes under other names to make a living. I have some resistance to the idea, I tell her, don't know if I want a stranger putting words in my mouth. I have enough ghosts in my past without having to hire one to tell my story.

The next evening, after I have completed a day's work only slightly less satisfying than the previous day's, I get a phone call from a writer who calls himself Joshua Quartz. His voice is so low I can barely hear him.

"What? What?"

"I've worked on commission," he says, "but I'd prefer a straight fee, half in advance, half on completion. Anything you say to me you don't want in the book remains in strictest confidence."

"To be honest, Joshua, I'm not terrifically happy having someone pretend to be me. Each step away from the source increases the falsification."

"You can dictate the story, and I'll write it in your own words."

"I can write it in my own words without you. Wouldn't you say? What I can't do is write it in your words."

Quartz does not try to sell me, says fine, leaves me his phone number and effaces himself. I admire the economy of his presentation, though also distrust it. Whatever manipulates, by definition, is manipulative.

His voice, it strikes me, has a pitch very similar to mine. Perhaps he is the son I never knew I had. I've always suspected Regina was pregnant when she walked out of my life.

Not the next day, or the next, but several weeks down the road, I find Quartz's number on the back of an envelope and call him on the spur of the moment. "I need some advice on my project," I say. "It concerns me that I'm not going to be around long enough to finish what I've started. So I'm going to need someone to translate my notes. If you're going to take over for me when I'm gone, it's important that you start working with me while I'm here. Do you see what I'm saying?"

"I'm into a novel," he says. "I don't really have the time to take this on."

"I'll pay you for your time," I say.

"What I'm doing means more to me than money."

"What do you say to a hundred dollars an hour for your time. Say fifteen hours a week. Say a guarantee of thirty weeks, though I suspect we can do it in half the time. Look at it this way, I'll be subsidizing your novel."

I can hear the air leak out of him. "I'll get back to you," he says. "This is a legitimate offer, huh?"

"We're talking a five thousand advance against a guarantee of forty-five thousand. Is that satisfactory?"

"You know it is," he says. "What made you change your mind about hiring me?"

"I'd rather not say, Josh, until we make some tracks together. I'd like you to start work right away if that's not inconvenient. Give me an address. I'll have a copy of my notes sent to you by messenger."

"I'll need a day or two to clear my desk. I'm thinking out loud now. Today's Monday. I'll get back to you with an answer on Wednesday. Anyway, I'd like to meet you face to face before taking this on."

"That won't cut it, I'm afraid. You're the man I want, Josh—as soon as I talked to you, I sensed a connection between us—but I don't have two days to lose. I'll need an answer by tomorrow morning. A meeting between us, I'm afraid, has no possibility. I see no one these days, not even myself."

"If that's the case, I'm going to have to say no," he says. "All right? I'm sorry." When he stays on the line, waiting for me to acknowledge his refusal, I know I have him.

It has been an adventurous afternoon for this recluse,my first day out in almost a month. In unobtrusive disguise—three weeks beard, short haircut, dark glasses—I find myself in this woman's unlived-in apartment, two maybe three blocks away from the East River. I am packing heat, my pistola in the right hand pocket of my leather jacket, prepared for virtually anything.

•

I met this woman, a post-hippie type in her early forties with frizzy hair, on a bench overlooking the river, and we struck up a conversation. Something in her odd manner—her uninsisted-on sincerity—allowed me to trust her. There was an immediate sympathy between us. I knew her the way a novelist knows a character he has imagined into being. She noticed that I was dressed inappropriately for the unseasonable cold and she kindly suggested I go with her to her place, which was only a few blocks away, to get a sweater her former husband left behind when he moved out.

She comes back into the living room, empty-handed, carrying nothing as if it were everything. She makes an elaborate, unnecessary apology. "The last time I was here, the closet was overrunning with his clothes," she says. "He must have gotten in somehow and taken them. There's, like, some stuff of mine that's also missing."

"That's okay," I say. "I'll phone for a cab." When I rub my hands together, they feel like strangers.

"The phone's been disconnected," she says. "I feel dumb bringing you here for nothing," she says. "Is there something I can do to make it up to you?"

It strikes me that there may never have been men's clothes in her closet and that her entire story has been a deception.

Instinct, the only advisor that doesn't lie knowingly, tells me I ought to leave, but she is appealing and I have not been with a woman since my break up with Camille.

She holds out her hand to me, a gesture out of a bad play, and leads me into the bedroom. No one wanting to deceive, I tell myself, would pretend to be such an unlikely person.

Matter-of-factly, she removes her silky purple shirtwaist and hangs it on the back of a chair. She wears no bra. Her breasts are exceptionally round, the nipple small and dark. I take off the lightweight leather jacket I am wearing, toss it inaccurately in the direction of a rocking chair on the far side of the room. The jacket falls like a weight, and I let out a sigh, remembering the gun in the pocket now lost to me. I am still fully dressed, though I feel uncovered, my secrets (which are next to nothing) given away.

"Take your pants off," she says, no stranger to authority. She is in the process of removing her black-striped gray tights, which had seemed painted on.

We have not yet touched. Is it excitement? I have difficulty catching my breath, hold my hand to my heart.

I remove my pants with more than usual reluctance. As you get older, you tend to be shy at facing judgment without the contrived dignity of costume. My stomach protrudes from under my shirt, asserts itself.

The ache in my chest seems from another lifetime.

"Would you like to lie down?" she asks.

I lean forward and kiss her left breast, which is sadder than the other, more in need of admiration.

"Most men tend to prefer that one," she says.

Not to be accounted one of the crowd, a partisan of mystery and surprise all my life, I brush the nipple of her right breast with the tip of my tongue.

"You're a gentleman," she says, taking command of the bed, establishing position on the side nearest the wall. As I move under the black comforter (speckled with tiny white flowers), I have the urge to confess something about my life."Hey, I'm hardly a gentleman," I tell her. "That's not what my life has been about."

She studies my face, holding me away at arm's length. "Standards have changed," she says.

"All I ever wanted was to find the ideal..." I hear myself say. She kisses me before the devious sentence is completed.

"My name is Rosetta," she whispers. "When you make love to me, I'd like it if you said my name."

"Rosetta."

"Yes, I like that," she says between kisses. "You're my sweetie."

I have the sense that there is someone moving around in the closet, a woman dancing among the clothesless hangers. It may only be the wind, which seems to rub itself against the window.

She is on top, her eyes closed behind her glasses, riding me. I say her name, which is hard to remember, which is gone from memory the moment it leaves my lips.

She sighs at the mention of her name, says: "Yes." And then, eyes open: "What do you like, Jack?"

I don't remember having told her my name is Jack.

"I like everything," I say, an odd remark, meant to be graceful. "Matter of fact, I like to be the one on top."

"Be my guest," she says. We turn around like one two-rumped creature.

"You're good, baby," she purrs. "I had no idea. Your wives must have been crazy to let you get away. Say my name, sweetie."

Did I tell her I had been married more than once? I don't remember.

Regina is the first name to come to mind, my first wife, my most passionately loved wife, the wife of my untried youth. I was crazy about her.

"Regina," I say.

1

Loss and Love Begin With the Same Letter

My first wife, the first of too many, my most passionately loved wife, announced one day in her most absolute voice that she couldn't live with me and she couldn't live without me. She made this meaningless, paradoxical comment moments before she left me after six years of marriage to return to her mother. I'd heard the statement before—everyone has—but what did it really mean? Was it a definition of love, of some kind of impossible love? We met on several occasions to discuss the issue, the final years of our marriage devoted to finding a way of coming apart with minimal sense of pain and regret. "What if I lived with you half the week and my mother half the week?" she asked. "That's crazy, isn't it?" She rejected her own suggestion before I had a chance to speak to its merits. Why not? I would have said. Still, I could see such a solution had limited duration at best. "What if you lived with my mother," she said, revising her suggestion, "and I lived alone in our apartment among your things? What bothers me most, Jack, is the idea of your having a life apart from me."

It was never easy to accommodate her. I offered to leave the country, to move some place where I would have no language. My former child bride liked that suggestion on the whole, though as she pointed out, the arrangement left certain of her needs unsatisfied. "There can be no other women," she said. "I couldn't stand it if I knew someone had replaced me. I know I have no right to ask that of you. That's something you would have to do without being asked."

I didn't think I could keep to such an arrangement, I confessed.

Regina sulked. She was wearing one of her wide-brimmed floppy hats—the purple one, as I remember—even though we were indoors. It was her way of sustaining mystery. "What hope is there for us?" she sighed. "There's no hope, Jack, unless you're willing to put selfishness aside and make some kind of commitment to the future."

The future spread out before me in its infinite blankness. "Okay," I said, accepting her reprimand. "Why don't we give ourselves two months and see if we can get it right this time. I mean, we've fucked up so much, maybe we've gotten the fucking-up part out of our systems. I'm willing to give it one last try, Regina, if you think there's any hope." I kissed the palm of her small chubby hand.

"Impossible," she said, blushing. "How can I live with a man who gives his own comfort and joy priority over mine? I realize now that I never loved you, Jack, never really loved you. That's the one thing I'm absolutely clear about."

The past slipped away as if it had never been. "I never loved you either," I lied.

We had reached an impasse, a new version of the old one. Regina crossed her arms in front of her, a gesture which usually meant trouble was on deck. "I love you, Jack," she conceded, "but the truth is I don't like you."

That cooked my potatoes. Her grievances, an excessive burden for her narrow frame, departed the coffee shop with her. That was the first meeting in a series of interminable, inconclusive negotiations.

"You have to stop bothering me, Jack," she said the next time we met. She had her hand in my jacket pocket at the time. "You had given me your word to stay away. If your word is no good, how can one trust you in more serious matters?" I reminded her that she had been the one to make contact, these meetings her idea. She waved her hand in a gesture of dismissal. "If you're going to throw irrelevancies in my face, how can we ever talk?" she said.

"I'm afraid I only have irrelevancies to throw at you," I said. "If I gave you jewels, you would say they were thorns."

"You've never given me jewels," she said, aggrieved. "So how would either of us know that?"

"Didn't I once for your birthday give you earrings with

some semi-precious stone?"

"More semi than precious," she said.

"That's not what you said at the time," I reminded her. "You said they were the most precious gift anyone had ever given you."

"What do you want?" she asked. "I'm open to hearing what you want. Here I am. I am available to you. Tell me what you want."

What did I want? "I want to get on with my life," I said.

"Well," she said, "that's not going to happen, Jack. Now can I say what I want. This is what I want since we're speaking our minds freely, more or less. What I really want is for you to disappear."

"I can't," I said. "I won't."

Our third meeting was postponed several times before it actually took place. She was cool this time—no fervent handshake, no flirtatious smile, no hit-and-run peck on the cheek. We met at the zoo, at the polar bear cage. She kept peering over her shoulder as we talked, as though she expected someone. It was like the scene in *Blow Up* where the Vanessa Redgrave character sets up a man to be assassinated. I didn't think of that at the time, had a different set of suspicions.

"It's your turn to come up with a solution to our mutual problem," she said, as if talking to the polar bear. "You have, if you don't mind my saying it, Jack, one of the most inventive minds I know. You really are terrific at creating disputes and then resolving them."

I basked in her sullied compliment, though I had nothing new to say, no new ideas, in a state of protracted emotional weariness. "We can study forgetfulness," I said at last, "though it has to be selective, you understand. There are things in this life I need to hold on to."

"I don't want to be forgotten," she said. "Don't forget me."

It was getting cold—the polar bear had retreated to its cave—and we went to my one and a half room apartment, a place we had spent the last eight months of our marriage.

In the apartment I had even less to say to her than I had at the zoo. When we sat on the couch next to each other, my prick announced itself, told me how things stood.

"Your silence is a form of withholding," she said, something her analyst had said to her about her own silence.

We got into a fight before separating for what I thought would be the last time, a physical fight that started with small bitternesses. "You always fail me," she said, punching me in the chest.

"The hell with this talk," I said. "Let's get to what this is really about."

"Never with you," she said. "I promise you we will never make love again." She shrugged my arm off her shoulder.

"You don't want to go to bed?" I said. "Is that what you're telling me?"

"I hope your prick drops off," she said.

"I think you mean that," I said.

When we fuck, that inevitable compromise with dead

feelings, it is like the tearing of flesh off corpses. There is no love, I hear myself think, without pain. I am married to pain.

"I can't," was what she said before and after, tearing at me with teeth and nails, her body limp and weightless like an inflatable toy. It was a nonnegotiable denial, unquestionably sincere. Denial freed her to pursue the impossible. It put her in touch with her need to rebel.

Regina, I discovered after several years of missing the point, was incapable of doing anything she had not already promised herself not to do. Before our marriage she told me that she couldn't marry anyone her mother didn't approve of, or anyone her mother actively recommended. The second category was of less concern. Her mother only advanced the suits of the deformed and dying, the palpably unlovable, men whose chronic discontent had become manifest in their physical presence. I may love you, she told me on several occasions, but I can never never marry you.

I took her at her word, recognized the hopelessness of my courtship, though did what I could to change her mind, sent her flowers, treated her badly, pleaded for forgiveness, refused to see her again. There was another man who also wanted or said he wanted to marry her, an older man she had known since she was ten, a friend (perhaps former lover) of her mother. His charm, in so far as I could tell from secondhand report, was that he had no charm, had negative charm. He also had a wife somewhere, a Catholic wife, who refused to give him a divorce. His ambiguous availability—he persistently offered what he couldn't deliver—made him, she confessed, almost irresistible.

I was young and penniless, had nothing to offer Regina beyond the boring insistence that I loved her, no prior unbreakable ties, no intractable flaws of character. I was not yet twenty, I was barely nineteen, I had no mystery. To see me—thin, surly, romantic, a secret swaggerer—was to know me to the heart.

I wooed her by refusing to see her until she broke off completely with my rival, the much older guy she referred to as her boyfriend. That's not exactly true. I saw her at times, but only when she pressed me to see her, would not take refusal, and each time only as a one time event never to be repeated. We met in secret at odd hours to discuss the impossibility of our situation. These trysts were unofficial and changed nothing. In the eyes of others (as we imagined the others imagining us) we remained a former item, a hopelessly broken-up couple. We both got off on the hopelessness of our passion, taking our sad pleasure, half-clothed, in the back seats of cars parked on deserted roads.

Each temporary separation presented itself as a final parting, each momentary goodbye the last time we would ever kiss. I knew it was love because it made no sense and wore me out. I knew we would go on this way forever; there was nothing to stop us. We had a private unspoken pact with the devil.

One day, in the back seat of a white Chevrolet, Regina said she would break off with her boyfriend (which always seemed the wrong word for a man almost old enough to be her father) if I would promise never to leave her. It was the night after the day she caught me walking with a former girlfriend, Tamarind Eckstein, in Central Park.

What did I know, what could I possibly know, about never leaving someone at nineteen? I expected to spend the rest of my life meeting Regina in the back seats of Chevrolets while the unloving world slept. That's love, isn't it? I knew the songs. To promise never to leave her seemed merely formalizing a commitment the heart had already made without recourse to the deceptions of language. I gave her the promise she asked for with only a moment or two of hesitation, something she would bring up to me in fights years later. In that momentary hesitation, she would let me know when the time was right, I had doomed our relationship forever.

The change in my status came gradually, remained our secret until Regina could bring herself to tell the deposed boyfriend of his fall from grace. It took awhile for her to find the propitious moment, that rare jewel of time. Weeks passed without her taking action. I suffered this period of inconclusion more intensely than anything else in our life together.

One night she called, sobbing uncontrollably, to tell me it was done and that he had taken it well. She was both happy and sad, her sadness inconsolable.

So I switched roles with the other man, the married older boyfriend with the compelling faults. I became the official man in Regina's life, and he became her secret. I didn't know that then, of course, and I don't know that for certain even now. It stands to reason, has its own unassailable logic.

I was happy to have won her, though felt unworthy, felt something was wrong. What was it that I wasn't seeing? I asked myself. All our talk was of how much or how little we loved the other.

Things seemed more fragile between us now. So we got married, rushed to marry as if our lives were parked at a meter, as if time or love would run out if we waited. We began our life together in a partially converted kitchenless garage, which was at the outer limit of what we could afford. I was working part-time while going to school, was busy all the time with one sort of make-work or another, seemed to see less of Regina after our marriage than before. The first year was the worst. We cluttered our inelegant garage apartment with grievances, outdid one another in wild accusations of heartlessness.

Regina brought to my attention that she was changing, evolving, from day to day while I was staying the same. And the more she saw herself change, the more stuck I appeared in intractable sameness. It was a cause for concern, an occasion for disappointment, a problem to be analyzed. The greatest cause of divorce in young marriages, she had read somewhere or had been told by someone whose opinion she trusted, was change. When you married as young as we had, if you didn't grow together, you were doomed to come apart.

Change represented mortality, and I resisted it. If we never changed, I pointed out, there was no way we could grow apart.

One morning, I woke to find her propped on an elbow, studying me. "You've changed," she said in an accusatory voice. "You're much more devious than you let on. You know that, don't you? Don't you?" She poked me in the side, tickled the bottoms of my feet.

I defended myself against her charges while apologizing for the very faults I denied. "What are you talking about?" I asked.

"You know," she said, adamant. "You know you know."

"I know I know what?" Said belligerently.

What I took mistakenly to be a fight turned out to be aggressive verbal foreplay. Regina sucked my prick, which let me know what she wanted, which was rare (since I was supposed to know without being told). In reciprocation, I worked my tongue up the inside of her thigh, took a circuitous route to her secret garden. That ended the discussion. For the moment, for that moment alone, I had passed her test.

She raised her head to say, "You're not so bad after all."

In the third year of our marriage—we were now living in a three-room, low-ceilinged attic above her mother's apartment—I came home early from work one day and discovered her in bed with her former boyfriend. Not in the act exactly, but seemingly directly after. They were smoking cigarettes and exchanging anecdotes about their lives. What else could it mean? "I told you, didn't I," she carped at him as I walked blindly into the room, "we should have gone to your place."

I backed out of the attic's only bedroom, wondering if I had stumbled into someone else's life story, if my three years with Regina had been nothing more than an extended dream. I considered the possibility that Regina and I had never reconciled, that she had married the other man—the unavailable aging boyfriend—instead of me. I sat in one of the standard-issue matching kitchen chairs with the imitation red leather seat, staring at the veins in my hands. Unless memory lied, I had woken up that morning in the double bed in the other room with Regina lying next to me in her black silky slip. That counted for something, didn't it? Still the evidence pointed in more than one direction. What I thought was my home was only the illusion of home. I had come home early, unannounced and unexpected, to find I had come to the wrong place. I was fitting the pieces together when the other boyfriend, dressed in a suit and tie, ambled into the kitchen. "You got to take better care of her," he said when I didn't acknowledge him. "That's if you don't want to lose her."

I stood up to show him that I was an inch or two taller.

"If you try to hurt me," he said, "I have some nasty friends who will come looking for you. There's no hiding from these guys. They know where to look."

"Get lost," I said, glancing at him with worked-up menace. He glared back, shook his head as if it pleased him to think me crazy, and hurried out.

I fell back into my chair, felt used up. Eventually Regina opened the bedroom door and made a tearful appearance. "Thank you," she said, eyes downcast. Thank you?

Her remark had its uncalculated effect. It threw me off, confused my anger. I may have said, "What?" I most likely said nothing at all. She came up close to me, as close as she could get without actually touching, her arms at her sides, rueful, sly. "Forgive me?" she asked in a little voice. "No," I said.

"I forgive you," she whispered. "Please forgive me.

Okay? What happened today was important to us, Jack. You claimed me. Today is the first day of our real marriage. You see that, Jack, don't you?" She reached for my hand, which moved into my pants pocket to escape her. "I love you more at this moment than I ever had."

"I won't forgive you," I said. There were tears in my eyes, which I hid (I thought) by keeping my face turned toward the wall.

She made a few more gestures of reconciliation, including burying her face in my lap, which I did my best to ignore, then went back to the bedroom in a sullen mood. "You'll be sorry," she said in an icy voice. "I promise you, you'll be sorry."

She left the door ajar, which was its own message. Would I be sorrier if I slipped inside, I wondered, or sorrier if I continued to play out the role of wronged party. I worried the issue until a decision one way or another seemed beside the point.

It was a little more than a year after that when she caught me in bed (it was a different place and a different bed) with a woman named Hannah, who had been a passenger in my cab. It was Regina's lunch hour, and she had come back to our apartment with a woman colleague of hers to pick up something she had forgotten. I was in the throes of coming, tuned in on my fast-receding pleasure, when I imagined I heard a key turning in the lock. Caught, frozen with remorse, I awaited discovery, prepared to deny the undeniable. The bedroom door never opened. Regina retrieved what she had come for in a matter of minutes, chattering to her friend in a strained clamorous voice that cut through me like a blade of ice. Suddenly she was gone. Reckoning would come later.

She didn't come home that night, went home, as she had before and would again, to her mother. When I called to present my case, she wouldn't come to the phone to speak to me. "How could you?" her mother said, a woman who disapproved of me from the start. "You don't know half the story," I said.

I waited three hours and called again and got the same off-putting result. During the afternoon of the next day, Regina was the one to answer the phone. She knew who it was before I cleared my throat. "I promise you I'll never return to you," she said after an extended silence. "That's over."

Her adamance defeated me. I offered an abridged version of my rehearsed speech, said I was sorry, said I missed her, two or three unrehearsed tears running down my face, an economy of grief.

"Give up on me," she said in the smallest of voices, waiting for me to disconnect.

A few days later, while I was out driving my cab, working later than usual because there was no one to come home to (I had given up on her as she had asked), she came back without prior warning. "I don't forgive you," she whispered to me in bed that night, sucking on my ear, her teeth like pinpricks. "I promise you I will never forgive you." She held on to me as though I were a port in a storm. I slept with her under my skin, our arms and legs hopelessly enmeshed.

I felt almost (all but) forgiven, my heart charred to ash. For days after that, we had no separate beginnings or ends. When Regina left the room for even a few minutes, I suffered her momentary absence like an amputation.

What was I to believe? I believed—the evidence had been accumulating—that I had decoded Regina's mystery. Her invitations invariably came disguised as rejections. That was her story. And (the inevitable corollary) her rejections presented themselves as assertions of undying affection. So when she announced one morning before I left for work—this, after six years of marriage—that she would never leave me, I should have known that she would be gone by the time I returned. Ah, but you see I didn't. Once again I willfully failed to read the text available to me. I let wishful thinking govern my behavior, let myself believe that in this exceptional case she meant exactly what she said. It was not that I didn't understand or had forgotten the all but predictable contradictions in her behavior. It was just that I didn't allow myself to know what I knew, didn't allow myself to read the emotional small print. Love obscures the text. The heart is the least literate of organs.

Our third meeting broke off after an hour; our fourth lasted three days, a period in which Regina moved in with me, warning me as it happened that it was not happening, that it could never happen.

"I don't know what's the matter with me," she said the morning of the third day. "I can't seem to leave you. I don't even know if you want me to stay."

I wasn't sure myself what I wanted, though I felt the

need to protect myself against the vagaries of Regina's behavior. "It's all right," I said.

"What's all right? If you want me to go, I'm not going to force myself on you," she said. "You have to make a commitment, Jack."

"I haven't asked you to leave," I said.

"That's because you haven't said anything, one way or another," she said. "What is it that you want, Jack? Commit yourself."

"I don't care anymore," I said. "I admit I like having you here, but I can handle it either way."

"If that's what you want," she said, her eyes slipping off, and I could see I'd entered the shadow world of ambiguity yet again.

Which of my statements was she responding to? That I wanted her to stay or that it didn't matter?

"I've just begun to find out what it is to love you," she said with a passion that was hard to disbelieve. Her assertion offered pleasure that translated almost immediately into anxiety. "What about you, Jack-o?"

"I've always known," I said, not knowing what I meant or what I knew. The next day she said in passing that if she was going to stay, she had to go to her mother's place to get some more clothes, and I said of course, but I knew it was a disingenuous ploy, an excuse to get away and not come back. I prepared myself for her not returning, anticipated disappointment.

When you anticipate disappointment—disaffection and betrayal—you are almost inured to its sting.

I did what I could to save myself. "Take your life in your own hands," my father used to advise on days when he seemed particularly beaten. I grabbed my life in both hands, sought out friends I hadn't talked to in years as a means of distraction. After packing the one dress and two pairs of panties she had left behind, I phoned Regina and told her not to bother coming back. She cried, was silent with tears, at her end of the tunnel. I hung tough, said I was sorry but that we had already played out our story. Giving her back her own words, I heard myself saying, "When love has gone there's no getting it back." What I didn't say was that I knew she had no intention of returning, was one step ahead of her this time around.

"You bastard," she said when she could catch her breath. "You'll regret this. I promise you, you'll regret it. Even when I said I loved you, I never loved you."

I had nothing to say to that, and she hung up before I could mouth whatever empty consolation the forked tongue contrived to offer.

I was exhilarated and vaguely miserable, was convinced (until Regina appeared at my doorstep that night) that I would not see her again, that I had taken my destiny in my own hands.

It was about midnight when she appeared and I was getting ready to go to bed, was brushing my teeth. She knocked at the door and when I didn't answer (the running water obscured the sound of her knock), let herself in with her key.

"I want you to know I forgive you for being pissy to me," was the first thing she said. The second was, "If you think I'm staying, one of us is crazy. That's a fact, Jack." She smiled slyly, stuck out her elegant tongue.

I translated her remarks as she spoke them, read her as if she were speaking a code to which I alone had the key. She was saying—I was sure this time I had gotten it right—that she wanted to resume our life together. The offer disguised the issue, made me forget my resolve.

"Sweetheart, I think we're going to make it this time," I said after we had kissed hungrily. "For sure," she said. We necked as if our not quite comfortable brown velvet sofa were the back seat of a car parked on a deserted road. It was old times with a vengeance, the same inexplicable stuff.

We forgave each other. I took her back. What else was there to do? We exchanged vows and fluids, blood flowed. Our lovemaking had the texture and implication of one of those treaties countries sign at the conclusion of wars. Fireworks went off in the distant heart.

"You're my baby," was the last thing I remember her saying before I entrusted myself to sleep. The difficulties of our marriage had all along been the source of its endurance. I saw clearly that this marriage was for good and, as lifetimes go, forever.

She slipped out during the night, never to return, while I slept like the dead.

2
The Soul of This Marriage is Brevity

It was one of those situations you read about in a certain kind of novel. I woke up one morning in a motel room and discovered I was married to the woman I didn't know tossing in her sleep next to me. A realist, I tried to make the best of it, thought I had as good a chance of making a life with this stranger as with anyone else. Her name—discovered by reading her driver's license, which she kept in a glassene folder in her wallet—was Lulu.

We pretended to know each other—a necessary illusion in a marriage—for almost a year, but it was a strain, such pretense. Our strangeness kept getting in the way. Only when we drank together, and only after an hour or so of drinking, did we seem to connect. "I know you," she would say. "You're the prick I married." "Lulu," I would say in response, "you're a fucking peach." When we sobered up, the next day or the day after, the nature of our connection remained a blurred shadow in memory, had less validity as experience than a movie I had seen the week before or a story someone had told me at a crowded party. The loss of those moments of intimacy kept me going, kept me in constant pursuit of the elusive.

One morning I woke up alone in a motel room I had never been to before, with a mostly empty bottle of bourbon on the pillow next to me, and I knew our marriage was over. When Lulu was gone I could barely remember her mean purple eyes and slightly lopsided Kewpie-doll face. The whole marriage seemed like one of those tantalizing dreams that fade to dust the moment you awake.

3

A Romance Forged in Low Light

You tend to marry the same woman in different disguise over and over again. That's what all the books on the subject say, though I am by nature a skeptic, and I have gone out of my way in this life to give the lie to received opinion.

My third marriage was what you would call a disaster almost from the start. You should never get married in low light—that's the lesson I take away. I met this woman—this older woman—in a bar in San Francisco. She looked vaguely familiar, which is what I remember saying to her. She thought the same about me. When we talked—I joined her in her booth—I felt an uncharacteristic ease with her as if we already knew the worst about each other, which we didn't. It was a month and a half to the day, a kind of anniversary, of the break up of my second marriage, and I was nostalgic and a little lonely. My eyes have never been very good at reading the mileage on faces. Anyway, even if she were a little older—I mean why should that matter?—I invited her to my hotel room, which happened to be across the street and also poorly lighted. It's a San Francisco thing, low lights.

We talked awhile, for hours, into the early morning and were mutually impressed with the similarity of our perceptions. We lived in the same world. Our secret passions corresponded to a remarkable degree. I don't remember whose idea it was—it may have been no one's idea, it may have been the conjunction of the stars—but ten days after we met we got married. I married this woman, who was older than I suspected, without even knowing her real last name. Two months into the marriage I learned the worst, what I thought at the time was the worst. It was immediately after sex—we were lying in bed together, smoking and free-associating. Mary Mags, as she called herself, was my mother's long lost younger sister, my missing Aunt Mary. It took me an unconscionable time to assimilate the troubling information, and even after accepting it, I continued to believe there was another explanation for the coincidence.

The secret out, our marriage seemed doomed to a few more shadowy months, a period for the most part of troubled silences and awkward avoidance. For awhile we tended to look in the opposite direction when the other came into the room. As time passed, we forgot what it was that made us shy with each other.

"At least," I said to her one morning, in a playful

mood, breaking the week-long silence at breakfast, "at least you didn't turn out to be my mother."

Her hands shot up in front of her face, foreclosed my view of her beautiful eyes. "The woman who raised you, the woman who indulged your worst habits, the woman you called 'mother,' I happen to know, was not your real mother."

This was the first I had heard of it. "If that's true, you're not my real aunt," I said. Most unhappy revelations had some consolation to them.

She nodded, her agreement ambiguous. "Jack," she said—she rarely called me by my name—"when I was fifteen I got knocked up. These things happened in those days, particularly on the west coast where the tides are more persuasive. Still, it represented disgrace, and we had to keep it quiet. Your mother, the woman you call mother, offered to bring up the child as her own as long as I took myself out of the picture, which I agreed to do."

Which one of us was it? I wondered. "What year was your child born?" I asked her.

"How old are you, Jack?"

"I'm twenty-eight," I said, which was stretching things. I was two months short of turning twenty-eight.

"When I told you I was thirty-five, I stretched the truth. The fact is, I'm in the neighborhood of forty-three. Please don't tell anyone my real age."

When you look at bad news closely it has a way of seeming worse than you had dared to imagine. I saw that there was no way we could continue this marriage without the worst kind of recrimination. We had to separate—that much was clear—but we liked each other so well, were so comfortable living together, we resisted coming apart.

Aunt Mary suggested that, having come this far as a couple, we finish out the winter together—the winter one of San Francisco's softer seasons. What was done, she pointed out, was inescapably done. "We have to learn to forgive ourselves," she advised me again and again, as if it were a new discovery each time the words came to her lips.

I was less comfortable with the relationship, was kind of anxious at this point to move on to something else, something less taboo, less psychically wrenching. We agreed to end our troubled marriage, but not right away, which I could see was a form of procrastination. Before we knew it, the days piling up like snow on the hood of a car, our second anniversary had come and gone.

For her part, Mary worked diligently—she had an unflappable quality which I've always admired—to give our lives the security of rarely-altered routine. She didn't like abrupt change, she said. Not liking our lives to change was one of the characteristics we had in common. Every Sunday morning, for example, she made it a point of bringing me breakfast in bed—blueberry pancakes, buttered scones, home fried potatoes, her own recipe scrambled eggs with bacon and sausages, a circle of orange slices guarding the border like a coat of arms.

She washed and ironed my shirts without being asked, wore them out with her relentless attentions. Aside from occasional nagging, her disposition was cloudless. She sang my praises and danced to my prospects, admired unequivocally the least of my gestures. It might rain outside, but inside our four and a half rooms the sun, in a sense, was always shining. A spotlight followed my every move. Aunt Mary went out of her way to make me feel like someone important.

Domesticity is an addiction like any other ritual comfort.

It was not that Mary was a wonderful cook—she had a predilection for too much flame—but she had two or three cunning dishes at her command that troubled the palate's memory years after their loss. Her singed meat loaf, when I think back on it, brings clutch to the throat.

We took each day as it came, followed the same basic thoughtless routines—rising and shining, showering, breakfasting, leaving home, returning home, dinnering, sleeping, rising and shining once again. Work, our separate jobs, filled the interstices. I was writing plays and painting other people's kitchens. Aunt Mary ran a small nursery school in the neighborhood. On weekends, I drove a cab.

We slept back to back like bookends.

We almost never fought in the life and death ways of more traditional couples. When Mary was upset with something I had done or omitted doing, I could always tell because she would put her hand over her heart, get this disappointed look on her face and leave the room like Hamlet's father's ghost.

I had a succession of bad dreams and tended to wake at two a.m. in the throes of heart-pounding anxiety. I bought a gun and took to shooting pigeons on a roof across the way to ease the panic. I started drinking at ten in the morning and didn't quit until sleep put me on the wagon for five hours or so. My headaches resisted the strongest of pain killers.

One night, unable to fall asleep at the usual time in the usual way, I put on my clothes over my pajamas (I tended to wear only bottoms), made myself a glass of hot milk laced with bourbon, and left the nest. I heard Mary call to me as I was sneaking out the door. "Take your cashmere scarf, dear," I think she said.

The next thing I knew the sun was rising, and I was on the road by myself with no possessions but the clothes on my back. I hitched a ride to the airport and took the first flight I could get, regardless of destination (I went to L.A.). Two days later, I went to San Diego, which I heard was a good place to disappear. I expected I would write Aunt Mary a note to explain myself, but I never got around to it. That isn't exactly true. I wrote a few letters—the same unacceptable excuses again and again—but I never found the occasion to mail them. Words are what got us into trouble in the first place. Words and indirect lighting, underwatted bulbs.

I had to believe Aunt Mary understood, though I have no real evidence for that assumption.

Years later when I would find myself in a poorly lit bar and see a woman of a certain age alone in a booth, I would be reminded of Mary and back out of the bar as if I had come to a wrong address. There was no need to repeat the same painful mistake twice, no matter how sympathetic or world-weary the older woman appeared.

I missed Aunt Mary for the longest time, which is normal according to all the books I've read on the subject.

4 Violence & Eros Make Common Cause

Make love not war.
Be prepared for both.
—sign on bumper sticker

After three failed marriages, in which large or small misunderstanding was generally the cause, I broke the pattern (or so I thought) by linking up with a woman who spoke virtually no English. We met at an audition for a movie about suicide and played a scene together, a love scene which turns on itself and becomes the occasion of a savage fight. The hostility of the characters we played seemed to carry over into our feelings for one another. She said something to me in French as we were leaving which, from the tone of her voice, I took to be disparaging.

"You're no bargain either," I said to her. "Speak English if you have something to say."

She said what I took to be the French equivalent of "Fuck off."

Still caught up in the violent scene we had performed, I pushed her away. She hit into a wall and seemed to bound back. I was looking the other way when she punched me in the eye. We rattled around the hallway of the studio, knocking each other about until a crew of guards separated us and threw us out.

I wanted to apologize for my violence, which was out of character, but she rammed her head into my mouth, and I bit my tongue.

We went to her place to continue our dispute. This agreement to continue our unpleasantness toward the other was made without words, was a matter of assumption and necessity. Isabelle lived in one room, one small room, in an out of the way development called Hollywood Villas. "This place is too small to fight in," I told her.

She seemed not to understand me, shook her head a few times, shrugged her shoulders. "Hey, cowboy, you are to me no good news," she said. "What is the way to the stars?" Then she rattled something off in French which seemed merely a restatement of her failure to understand.

"How can you not know what small is?" I said. I held up thumb and forefinger with less than an inch in between.

She slapped my face, and was about to a second time when I blocked her with my forearm. "Au revoir, mes enfants," I said, one of three French expressions I had at my command. "I'm cutting out, going home, taking a hike, getting out of your hair."

I noted to myself that Isabelle, who had a wretched complexion, her face pocked like the moon, had a sexy mouth.

She bumped me with her shoulder, and I bumped her back, then she butted me in the stomach. I kissed her wonderful pout of a mouth, and she bit my lip drawing blood. There was no place to move without bumping into something with sharp edges. I was afraid to hit her again, though the bloody lip infuriated me.

The advantage of hitting her was to occupy her in self-defense. What I did as an alternative tactic was wrestle her to her bed and hold her down by putting my full weight on top of her. My strategy was to leap up while her attention was diverted, so I might get away without making myself available to further assault. She undulated against me, a distraction which undermined my intention. I became aware, inescapably aware—her nipples were erect—that she wore no bra. I had a sorry hard-on.

"Biche," I said to her, which I somehow imagined was the French word for bitch. "I'm going to make you sorry you ever took me on."

"Non," she said, trying to rip off my ear with her teeth.

In turn, I tried to rip out her teeth, dislodge her jaw, which she countered by biting my hand. We hardly knew each other, and yet we couldn't stop fighting. I tried to escape, kept pushing her down on the bed and pulling myself up. But she was too quick for me and grabbed me from behind each time before I could get away, her arm snaking around my neck as though she meant to choke me. She wore an intoxicating perfume.

Our groins, clenched like fists, pounded each other.

Between bouts of fighting, as a kind of interlude, we got into fucking, which she worked at with the same savage passion as the fighting. Occasionally one or the other of us would fall asleep, too exhausted to sustain either of our major activities. When we recovered we immediately continued whatever we had been doing, the fighting or fucking whichever it was. When I collapsed into sleep, I tended to pull myself awake after five or ten minutes, afraid of losing control, afraid of being killed while I slept, struggling to maintain consciousness like a drowning man.

Days passed. My main concern, my one abiding obsessive concern, was to get out of her tiny apartment and go home. But it didn't happen, continued not to happen, I couldn't seem to find the will or the heart to get myself through the door. The dynamic of our relationship occupied me. This was my story, my life. I wanted to find out what was going to happen to us next. You can't turn the page if you've already closed the book.

On the third day we ran out of what little food she had. The last of the frozen pizzas had been scarfed down. I was hungry, and I needed a change of clothes. While she was sleeping, I dragged myself out of her closet of an apartment, her tomb-like space, and got into my car, which didn't start at first (everything was in conspiracy against my escape), which only started when my hopes for it had all but vanished, and stole away.

In the bathtub I checked out my bruises and recognized I was lucky to escape this relationship without crippling injury. Another week together and one of us might have done permanent damage to the other. My wounds were a topographical map of my mortality.

Two weeks later, my strength partially recovered, I went back to Hollywood Villas to see if Isabelle was all right. As truce offer, I was bearing a dozen white roses and a frozen pizza. When she didn't answer my knock, I left my gifts on her doorstep. I worried that she had neglected looking after herself in my absence. As I turned to go, I heard the door open tentatively behind me.

I remember the moment as if it happened in slow motion and I was watching it on a screen. I delayed turning around, wasn't sure what she looked like, had lost all record of her face. I think I was embarrassed at the prospect of not knowing her, at having no words to explain why I was there. She glanced at me, then looked away before I could catch her eye. She was studying her hands. "I came back," I said, a confession of the self-evident.

She said something incomprehensible in reply—a mix of French and oddly-pronounced English—that I took to be a statement of indifference. I saw that she had an astonishing face and that she was shy and embarrassed. I saw that I loved her.

"What is it you may want?" she said as if it were something she had memorized incorrectly from a phrase book.

"I came back because I had to see you," I said with melodramatic passion.

She went inside without a word, leaving the door open behind her. I took it as an invitation to follow. Her depressingly small apartment had not grown in my absence.

The prospect of continuing our fight aroused me, though also produced anxiety. I bumped her gently with my shoulder to no avail. She cried, pulled at her hair, pushed me away when I pulled her to me.

"*Qu'est-ce que c'est?*" I said, hoping it was the right question.

Her answer was to shove in my face an official letter she had gotten from the immigration bureaucracy.

It took me awhile to penetrate its bureaucratic language. As near as I could understand its implications, Isabelle had to get either a job or an American husband within two weeks of the date of the letter, which was the day after tomorrow or else be subject to deportation. My decision made itself on the spot. I had no job to offer her, so I proposed marriage, proposed that she marry me in order to beat the system. I thought, Well, we could always get a divorce afterward.

I don't know what she understood, but she said "*oui*" which I knew to mean yes, then she laughed and kissed me on both cheeks. I lifted her off the ground, and she wrapped her legs around my waist. Our foreheads bumped. We shared pain. Later she bit me on the neck with her small sharp teeth, a love bite, drawing blood.

Her nails raked my back.

It may not have been that way, not exactly like that. My memory tends to focus on the extreme, on the pleasure disguised as pain. What is undeniable is that we got married three weeks to the day after we auditioned together for a part in a movie. My joke, which she failed to understand, was that we had entered into a marriage of inconvenience.

We performed our parts in this inconvenient marriage better than I would have thought possible. Isabelle got a job as a waitress in a French restaurant while waiting to be discovered. I got a job revising screenplays for porno films, for which I showed real flair. Then I got a role in a legitimate movie, a speaking part with nine words. Only one word and a long shot of my back survived the final cut.

We kept a French/English dictionary in almost every room, though we rarely found occasion to use them. I think we both got off on the silences. That we didn't rely on words made us immune, in a certain sense, to misunderstanding. Sex was our common language, sex and whatever came in its trail. She sang to me in bed in French, songs about yearning and sadness, cries of bottomless despair. For a while, until we began to understand each other, I couldn't get enough of her. We had a game in which she would punch me in the shoulder and run off. I would count to ten before pursuing her. We would end up fucking wherever I happened to catch her, on the very spot. It was the unspoken rule of the game.

For the first three or four months, this was my most rewarding marriage—the kind of marriage one might want to recommend to everyone. Mysteriousness is the answer, I thought. Passion is all, is everything, is nothing if not everything. We made love in the bathtub, on the cracked leather couch, in two different closets, on the living room rug, under the bed, on the kitchen table with our legs hanging over the side, wherever impulse took us. In one of our games, I had to bite her toe to win her favor, which meant holding her down at the same time. This was almost impossible without acquiescence on her part because even after I caught her, which was hard enough, I had to force her to the ground and hold her in place while I removed her shoe. Sometimes I would end up getting kicked in the mouth for no other reason than it was in range of her foot. But when I won her on these terms, when I bit her toe, there was nothing ever as good as what followed. I loved her murderous abandon, kisses with teeth, caresses with claws.

What went wrong, along with the ordinary disaffections that familiarity is heir to, had to do with Isabelle learning English. It was unavoidable, one of the side effects of being a waitress in Los Angeles. I could see the danger coming, but there was nothing I could do to head it off.

Every day she was learning more, understanding more. In the beginning it was exciting to hear her do violence to language. But I tired of her prattle after a while. Day by day, as if decoding herself, she lost a little more of her mystery. As she understood me better, she also became less enthralled with me.

"You are never listen to me," she would complain, when it seemed to me that the other way around was more nearly the truth. It was she who never stopped talking long enough to hear what I had to say, which in those days wasn't much. Over dinner, which was usually take-out, we exchanged stories about the day's events. Isabelle used the occasion to showcase her improved English, would parade out the latest witless cleverness she had picked up in the restaurant that day and almost mastered, would offer it with an ingenuous faith in its power to amaze. I would nod appreciatively and applaud. The applause, it turned out, was never as much as she felt she deserved. And when I clapped until my hands ached, she took it for irony and was even more dissatisfied than before. "You don't know what kind of woman you've got," she would say from time to time, and I would say, "but that's the point, isn't it?" And of course she didn't understand what I meant, hadn't the faintest idea. "I couldn't care less" was her favorite locution, her most tireless wisdom.

We were lonely together. As we understood each other more, the spaces between us enlarged. Our passion didn't diminish, but had become a secret parody of itself. We made love every night. It had become an obligation to human survival like eating and sleeping and going to the movies. Lovemaking had become the self-prescribed medicine of our failing marriage. We couldn't care less.

Respectability, as I see it, ruined us, the stultifying repetitions of domestic life. Isabelle developed a sudden passion for the appropriate. "We must do our things like other married people," she would say to me in bed. Fighting as prelude to fucking was no longer acceptable behavior. Physical violence was anathema to the respectable. We pursued propriety, the forms of propriety, as if the future of civilization depended on us. "The husband is caring to the wife," she would remind me from time to time. When we stopped fighting altogether, something died in us. I think it was the memory of passion that died. We stopped chasing each other around the apartment. Our most compelling routine had become off limits.

"You do not will to do things right," she lamented one morning in bed. "You don't want people to know you are nice guy so you behave like the savage."

"I do my best to give that impression," I admitted.

"No, you do not do your best," she said, misunderstanding me. "If you do your best, it will be different. Success in life will beat a path to your door."

"My doors will remain locked," I said. "Success will never get its beaten path into my house."

That stopped her momentarily. "You are being silly, yes?" she said.

"Yes," I said. "Silliness is the last refuge of the unregenerate savage no longer allowed his savagery."

"Are we happy?" she asked me on another morning, not wanting my answer, not waiting for it. "I think yes," she mused while I gave the question a moment of distraction. "Sometimes I think no, sometimes I think yes. I would give up everything to be happy all the time."

The more she talked the more I realized she was not the person I married.

How could I have been so deceived? I would ask myself as if something in me had the answer.

The fall out of love (it was as if someone had pushed me out a window again and again) left me feeling cheated and misused.

On Saturday nights it was our routine to go to the movies. We would see whatever was at our neighborhood theater, which happened to be two doors down the street. We went faithfully—they changed the show every Wednesday and, expecting to like nothing, we were rarely disappointed. We took particular pleasure in trashing the performances of actors whose roles we coveted. As with most of our extended conversations, the language barrier precluded subtleties. Consequently, each discussion, no matter the movie, no matter the actress or actor, became the same discussion in barely discernable variation. This was the last area in which we remained more or less of the same mind. The rest was disparity and misunderstanding and despair.

I never actually told her that I missed the times that we chased each other around the apartment and made love—fucked—wherever the chase completed itself. While it was happening, it didn't require acknowledgement, and when it was over it no longer mattered. I never told her that she had a sexy pout of a mouth and that I missed bruising my mouth against hers. I never told her that I loved her shy silences, her eloquent stammering silences, which were lost to language, lost forever.

I didn't wait for the inevitable end. One day, after a routinely good night of respectable lovemaking (the savage subtext never disappeared altogether), I took a taxi to the airport and got on the first available flight to New York. I left both my career in movies, which would come in its own time, and Isabelle (the Isabelle who had become someone else), and went home to my first home. I gave up fast-fading illusion and illusory respectability to return to the hallucination it pleased me to think of as the real world. I sent a letter of explanation and some money("marriages of inconvenience have to end when they become convenient," I wrote), and asked to have my clothes sent on. They arrived ten days later, without a note, drenched in her perfume and cut to shreds.

5

Answering a Call for Love

I got into reading the Personals in the back of *The New York Review of Books* as a form of idle fantasy. It was a period in my life in which nothing satisfied me. I was looking for something—some experience or relationship—that I had been incapable of imagining, something elusive and inconceivable. Even if I was not so naive as to take the Personals at their word, I nevertheless was intrigued by what a woman behind a particular ad was like, wondered how much discounting the reader had to do to get to the real thing.

My fantasies were whetted by women who presented themselves as having a Renaissance range of alliterative graces: soulful, sensitive, soft-hearted seductresses, conversant with the Beatles, Balanchine, Bach, baseball and bliss, dark, diminutive dancers who read Dostoyevsky, Derrida, Dante and Doonsbury, independent, intuitive, insightful icons inured to inanity, open to touching, tenderness, technology, and Trivial Pursuit, casually charming catatonics into Cheers, Cherry Garcia, conversations by candlelight, chortling, carpe diem, Chinese cinema and conjugal commitment in the same sentence. The reason I hadn't answered one of these ads, apart from a kind of free-floating inertia, was that the rhetoric daunted me. In my tattered human clothes, I was not worthy of any of these paragons, not then.

This is the ad I finally answered. "I am not particularly beautiful or interesting. I have always been sad without knowing why. The truth is, there is little special about me. I am smart enough to know I am fairly shallow and lack imagination. Would like to meet a man aware of his limitations. Only the unillusioned need apply."

How could I resist? I wrote back a short note saying that she sounded like my kind of woman, and suggested we meet. I gave her my phone number.

She didn't answer right away, and I wrote again saying that I had a strong sense that I was the man she was looking for. My unillusionment was without flaw.

In my third letter I wrote, "Look, you started this by advertising. The least you can do is check me out."

For a while every time the phone rang I expected it to be her, rehearsed a reply before picking up the receiver.

When two months had gone by (I had written another letter, an angry one), I accepted the fact that I had failed her test. I accepted my limitations grudgingly.

I was at home, cooking dinner for a woman I had been seeing off and on—in the middle of things—when the phone rang.

"I don't know what you want from me," a voice said, a woman's voice, though it could also have been a man's.

"Who is this?"

"No one," she/he said, "who do you think it is?" and hung up.

I thought it had been a wrong number until an hour later when it struck me—I was in bed with the woman I had cooked dinner for—that I had finally gotten the call I had been waiting for. Instead of giving up on her—the lesson of her difficulty had already been taught—I wrote once again (this I told myself was the absolutely last time) and suggested a meeting at the Cedar Tavern on University Place. I said that I would be there at such and such a time, dressed in such and such a way, sitting at such and such a table. I asked her to wear something red, but said that I would recognize her regardless.

The woman (her name, Cara Lou) did show up for our meeting, though not quite on time. I want to get that out of the way so that I can get to the real issues and not prolong an irrelevant suspense.

She was large; no, she was very large. That was the first thing one noticed about her, her hugeness, which seemed magnified by her red cosmic tent of a dress. She was six feet tall and must have weighed close to three hundred pounds.

I wanted to defend her from the obvious shock on my face. "Please sit down," I said, but she hesitated, and I realized that the chair was not wide enough to hold her. I stood up and shook her hand.

"You're not what I expected," she said, "and I'll bet I'm not at all what you expected. I want you to be honest with me."

"I had no expectations," I said, which was a lie. I was offended by her size, felt her ad had been a willful deception.

"The reason I didn't answer right away," she said, "is that I wanted to lose a little weight before you saw me."

We had a drink and hors d'oeuvres (I drank and ate while she sipped and nibbled), and then I drove her home. She had a skittish manner, was quick to take offense. I was as gallant as I knew how to be, held doors for her, treated her like a princess.

"I don't like to invite people in on the first date," she said, and I made no effort to persuade her otherwise.

We went through an elaborate ritual of saying goodnight and shaking hands (it went on for ten minutes or so). Like this:

"Thank you for answering my Personal," she said.

"My pleasure," I said, taking a small step backwards.

"You're a lot nicer than I expected you'd be," she said, holding out her hand and withdrawing it. "I had a nice time. Even if it didn't seem that way, I really did."

"That's nice of you to say," I said, shaking her hand for the second or third time.

"If we get to know each other better," she said, "which will probably never happen, well who am I to say, I hope maybe you'll come inside if I ask you."

"Goodbye, Cara Lou." We shook hands again.

"I hope I haven't said the wrong thing," she said. "My sister always says I don't do anything without putting my foot in my mouth. Do you think she's right?"

"I haven't heard you say anything wrong."

"Oh thank you," she said, holding out her hand.

"Well, goodbye then."

And finally I escaped to my car with the not unhappy assumption that I would never see her again.

"You have a beautiful face," I said to her in a dream. "I'm in disguise," she said, "but you know that, don't you?" I didn't know what I knew. I called her two days after the dream and invited her to dinner at my place. She turned me down, though stayed on the phone.

"If I ask you to dinner again, are you going to turn me down again?" I asked at the apparent conclusion of our aimless conversation.

"You won't ask again," she said, with impressive assurance. "Thank you for asking me."

The formality of her manner touched me.

She continued to turn down my invitations to dinner and I continued, not expecting to be accepted, to make them.

She wouldn't come to my apartment, but at some point she invited me to dinner at hers. How could I say no?

"I'll make you a deal," I said. "I'll go to your place if next week you come to mine."

"I won't," she said.

There was another couple there, which was the first of several surprises. The second and more notable surprise was the spaciousness and splendor of her town house. The place was filled with art objects (mostly Japanese)—masks and lacquered boxes—and what I assumed were antiques, fragile sticks of furniture from some other world and time. I had expected Cara to be living in some dowdy, self-deprecating way. The self-consciousness of the place, not to mention its elegance and wealth, shattered almost all my preconceptions about its owner.

There was a servant—a Japanese with a scar above his lip—who cooked and served the food.

It was not until we sat down at the dinner table that Cara Lou introduced me to her other guests, a look-alike couple (both very thin and overdecorated) called the Colemans. They tended to ignore me or to condescend to me, and I strove to give them back their own.

Cara Lou floated about, with a child's smile on her lush face.

When I caught her alone I whispered to her that I hadn't expected this dinner to be so grand. She said, "Thank you," and blushed.

The other couple left as soon as dinner was completed, the woman (who was Cara Lou's sister) making elaborate apologies before rushing out. So I was alone with Cara Lou except for the cook who had receded into the depths of the apartment.

This is what happened.

We sat next to each other on a wicker sofa in one of several sitting rooms and after a few words of awkward small talk fell into silence. Then, as one thing follows another with an inevitability that denies choice, we began to kiss. Her lips were sticky.

It was like the second of my three dreams about her. The necking was not a preliminary to something else (to real sex, for example), but the main event, the only event.

"I like you," she confessed.

"I like you too," I said.

"Not the way I like you," she said.

I was thinking it's time to go but I said nothing, made no move to leave, waiting for her to dismiss me. "This is what I thought it would be like," she said. "What about you?"

I told her about kissing her in my dream. "Yes," she whispered.

I announced that it was time for me to leave, and she said in an absurdly serious voice that she knew that. Separating had the texture of a kind of mourner's ritual. It was as if, once apart, we would never have occasion to see each other again. But another dinner invitation came—this one by mail—and I accepted, didn't know how not to accept. I was intensely aware of her vulnerability and so felt obliged not to take advantage of it. I was teaching myself to be kind.

I went to a second "dinner party" two months later in which the same other couple also appeared—and also disappeared moments after the meal. This time the woman deigned to talk to me. She said, "You and Cara Lou are becoming quite an item."

"I don't understand what you're saying," I said.

She laughed with what I took to be scorn. "I bet you don't, blue eyes," she said. "I just bet you don't."

Later, when we were necking, I said to Cara Lou I didn't understand why her sister didn't like me.

"Pegeen thinks all men are after is my money," she said. "You don't care about my money, do you?"

"I hadn't thought about it," I said, which was the moment's truth.

I also had another girl friend at that time. I think it's important to mention it before we get too much further. Chronically discontented, sexy Valerie knew about Cara Lou, but Cara Lou had no idea of the existence of Valerie, which is to say I had never mentioned Valerie to her. Of course Cara Lou might have suspected something. Cara Lou was a surprising person, seemed at times to know things in a certain way she had otherwise no reason to know, which I thought of as a kind of extrasensory perception. So it's possible she sensed something even then, knew in her childish private way what she had no way of knowing through the usual sources of information.

On our fourth evening together, she made me an astonishing proposition. She was dying, she said, had at most five years to live (probably less). What she wanted—it took her awhile to shape the words—was to marry me. She didn't mention that she was very rich and that she would leave me her money when she died, but that was implicit in the offer.

"Don't answer right away," she said in response to my silence. "Think about it, okay?"

I said nothing at first in answer to her unacceptable proposition, could think of nothing to say that would not be hurtful to her. I hoped my silence would be sufficient refusal.

"Okay?" she asked again.

I said I would have to mull it over.

I made the mistake of mentioning Cara Lou's offer to Valerie who, after an initial show of outrage, became obsessed with the idea. For the next few times we were together, it was her only subject. "What's your latest thinking on Cara Lou's proposal?" she asked, a trace of irony in her manner. "Which way is the wind blowing?"

"There's no wind," I said. "The whole thing's out of the question."

Valerie, in an angry (perhaps ironic) mood, encouraged me to marry Cara Lou. "I don't see how you can say no," she said. "I mean, it's for the greater good, isn't it?"

I thought all along that Valerie was being ironic, but then it struck me that she also meant it. Why else did she hold onto the issue so long? "Whose greater good?"

"It's a boon for everyone, Jack, don't you see that? She gets what she wants, you get what you want, and maybe even I get what I want in the longish run."

"I'm not going to do it," I said.

Cara Lou was at my place—her first visit there—when I gave her my long-delayed answer to her proposal. "I've gotten very fond of you, as you know," I started out by saying.

"I know that," she said. "I also know that you don't really love me."

Her remark flustered me, and I was unable to continue. Some response was necessary, but I didn't want to lie or didn't want to seem to lie. "What do you think you know?" I said.

She put her hand over my hand in a protective gesture. "Don't mind me," she said. "I'm not smart enough to say the right things."

"You always say what you mean," I said. "I like that you don't lie."

"I'm a terrible liar really," she said. "I interrupted you

before. Continue what you were saying if you don't mind."

The interruption had, if not changed the course of my intention, muddled it somewhat. "I can't accept the terms of your offer," I said.

"You don't want to marry me?" The question asked as if heartbreak were at issue.

"I didn't say that," I said.

"You will marry me?"

I realized then that I wasn't going to refuse her, didn't have the heart or the legs or the will. I said something about not being interested in her money, and she said she understood because she wasn't interested in her money either.

Cara Lou hugged me with passionate enthusiasm, hugged the air out of me, and we had a pact, the presumption of a pact I immediately regretted. We were, so to speak, engaged.

I thought Valerie would be pleased since she had been a partisan of the marriage, but when I told her, she was disheartened. "I'll miss our times together," she said.

"I'll still be able to see you," I said. "Things won't change that much."

She gave me an out-of-character censorious look, said, "I don't go out with married men."

Now I didn't want to lose Valerie, who was terrific in bed, inventive as hell, funny and sexy, imagined myself off-and-on in love with her. "Why did you advise me to marry her?" I said in complaint.

"Because I'm a fool," Valerie said and threw herself under the covers, masking her face with the sheet. I lay down next to her, removed the sheet, stroked her damp face, kissed her breasts, worked downward, sucked her stomach, played out the best tricks in my game. Still she was adamant afterward about not seeing me again. "You made your choice," she said. Then she ate me for old times' sake and pushed me out of bed. "You can let yourself out, Jack."

The wedding was held at Cara Lou's house and was conducted by an apparent friend of the family (one of few from what I could tell) and kept inordinately short. There were six guests in all, including me. The reception was both modest and excessive. There wasn't much—three bottles of vintage champagne, a few trays of hors d'oeurves—but it was all the best of its kind money could buy. When it was gone—it seemed to happen in the blink of an eye—the guests, including the friendly minister, were gone with it.

Since I was the husband now, I was obliged to stay, which was not anything I was prepared for. When we were alone—necking seemed somehow inappropriate given the new terms of our relationship—we played board games. Stratego was Cara Lou's favorite, and we played it over and over again, each trying to let the other win, until we could no longer keep our eyes open.

I spent part of my wedding night on the living room floor, my head against Cara Lou's knee. Then we went to bed, Cara Lou in her room, the husband (a role I had trouble getting into this time around) in the bedroom at the far end of the long hall.

"Don't we get to sleep in the same bed?" I asked before going off to my assigned place.

"Only if we want to," she said.

I didn't pursue the question, went to sleep in my separate room.

I didn't know at the time that Cara Lou was a virgin, hadn't addressed the question to myself.

The next night, after two games of Monopoly and one of Othello, she whispered in her sexy little girl's voice, "They might want to occupy the same bed tonight, Jack. What do you think?"

"They might," I said. "I think it's a likely possibility."

She embraced me, and we necked awhile in our premarital way, then holding hands tightly, we walked slowly (like figures in a suicide pact) into Cara Lou's bedroom. The room was furnished like a monk's cell, though was large enough to house a small monastery of monks. Its centerpiece was a larger than king-sized platform bed, which gave the impression of being a small stage in the midst of a larger one. There was one picture on the wasteland of white wall, a Renoir drawing of two voluptuous women, which I later learned had been a gift from her father who had moved on to another wife when Cara Lou was thirteen. Cara Lou asked me to turn my back while she undressed, which I did, and when I turned around ten minutes later—my patience greater than usual—she was under the covers, her hands clasped in front of her like a schoolgirl waiting for teacher to begin the lesson.

Consummation took longer than I expected, took longer

than anyone who had not been there might have imagined. It was a combination of problems, her enormous size the major obstacle to our pleasure, coupled with our mutual indifference to conclusion. There was no rush, no appointments that had to be kept (I had a tryout for an avant-garde play about two brothers that kidnap a derelict whom they make over into a version of their father that I let pass), nothing to get us out of bed without finishing what we seemed barely able to start.

We stayed in bed for three nights and two days, working in good faith toward our common end, fucking around like teenagers (like fucking children), while negotiating how to fuck like adults. I liked it best with Cara Lou on top, which was otherwise not my usual cup of tea, though we couldn't connect that way for more than a moment at a time. Her soft weight dissolved me, took away my breath. We got it going on the second day (a variation on an arrangement natural to dogs) and, having learned the trick, rehearsed it, off and on, through the night. It was better than Stratego, as Cara Lou said. For my part, there was more pleasure in the preliminaries—it was her innocence that got to me most—than in the end game, the child-making game itself.

With the sex out of the way, my basic responsibilities temporarily fulfilled, I was free to pursue my other business, my stuttering career as a man of the theater. I continued to make cast calls for off-Broadway plays and took a three night (sometimes all night) a week job driving a cab, which left me afternoons to audition. I suggested to Cara Lou that she get some kind of work outside of the house, but she said that work had never interested her.

For three weeks, perhaps a month, except when the sister and look-alike husband came to dinner, we were more or less happy. We were surprisingly happy. Our days were careless. We lived like wayward children together in a paradise of luxury.

Valerie, who had vanished even from memory, called one day and said, "Your absence from my life saddens me. Isn't there some way we can remain friends?"

I was pleased to hear from her—I admit that—but I said, "I don't think I can manage it."

"I get what you're saying," she said. "If it weren't for me, you know, you never would have married her."

I put her off, did what I could to discourage her (told her I loved my wife), but she kept after me, called, wrote letters, made whimsical threats, reminded me of promises I had never made.

One day she arrived at our town house and introduced herself to Cara Lou as my sister. She was wearing a large red backpack over one arm, her overnight kit.

"I don't want her to stay," I whispered to Cara Lou.

"I like her," Cara Lou whispered back. "I really really like her."

Valerie made up some elaborately incoherent story about travelling around Europe for five years and then waking up one morning with a passionate desire to return home, home being where the heart was.

Cara Lou said, "This is your home for as long as you want to stay with us."

The three of us had dinner together in the formal dining room (I was the only one who was silent), and Valerie was ensconced in a room just down the hall from me, a room between Cara Lou's and mine. All of this, I had to know, invited trouble. Trouble, in a manner of speaking, had invited herself.

It was not the first night but the second, when trouble visited me in my bed in the early hours. "We need to talk," trouble said, getting under the covers alongside me.

"I'll talk to you," I said, "but not here, not like this."

She pressed herself against me. "This is the only way I can get your undivided attention."

"Cara Lou is a light sleeper," I said, not meaning the pun, unaware of it until the words floated from my mouth. "I'm asking you out of basic decency to go back to your room."

"No," she said.

We wrestled. I lifted her from the bed, carried her to the door, struggled to open the door. (What was I going to do with her when I got her into the hall?)

"I'll scream so loud it will blow the walls down," Valerie whispered. "How will you explain that to your light sleeper?"

I offered to settle, took her back to bed in exchange for a promise to leave the next day. It was an exchange of convenient deceptions, an agreement between liars. We faced each other in bed, propped on elbows, like unacknowledged enemies seeking a subtle advantage. When we kissed—I have no idea who made the first move—I had a premonition of what it might be to visit my death. We fucked on the dark side of the moon.

"It's not the way it was," she said.

It was better and worse, was suffused with a shuddering sense of the unforgiveable.

Her orgasm was like one of those car alarms outside

your window that you think will never stop. I put my hand over her mouth. She kissed my palm. The heart, which had died, returned to life.

She didn't leave the next day, which in truth was no surprise. "You made a promise," I reminded her when we were alone, Cara Lou in her room, Cara Lou a secret person.

"Did I?" she said. "I don't remember promising anything." She gave me one of her best seductive smiles, a state of the art sexpot smile. "Was it good for you last night?" she murmured. "Do you still love me a little?"

I didn't have a chance to answer because Cara Lou came up on us to announce that dinner was about to be served. It was more than possible that she had overheard our conversation.

Cara Lou hummed while she ate, was in particularly good cheer.

That night in Cara Lou's room, I said that I thought it might be helpful to Valerie—she had a tendency to drift—if we urged her to find her own place.

"I feel that your sister is my sister," Cara Lou said, oblivious to my point. "I'm so happy, Jack, that she's agreed to stay with us. It fills the gap."

"What gap is that?" I asked, my face between her enormous breasts, cushioned against the prospect of impending disaster. Was I behaving inexcusably? I wondered. Was I happy? Was happiness the issue?

As she went on, describing her sisterly feelings toward Valerie, their sudden blooming friendship, and then how lonely she had always been, how friendless, I saw there was nothing I could say to make her believe (nothing that wouldn't discredit me in her eyes) that we would all be happier with Valerie elsewhere.

"She may have to leave one of these days," I said. "She has her own life."

"I don't want her ever to leave," Cara Lou said in a child's voice. "I want you to convince her to stay."

There was more of the same, Valerie's name (and so her presence) never quite leaving the arena. She loved Valerie as much as she loved me, she said without saying, loved Valerie because of me. There was no way of changing her mind without letting out the truth, and it was too late for that. The truth, at this point, would embarrass us all, would smash everything.

I got a part in a play, which was excuse to stay out of the house for longer stretches of time, though Cara Lou, unlike former wives, never asked me to account for my time away. I revised my taxi-driving schedule to include all day Saturday and all night Thursday. I was rarely home, which was a way of limiting opportunity for trouble.

Valerie seemed to look for work when the mood took her, checking off ads in the paper, making the occasional phone call, but on the whole it was an activity without conviction, just another way of disappointing hope.

She came to my room three or four nights a week (usually between one and two a.m.) in a succession of sexy nightgowns—a different one each time as if a different self were being offered. I seduced her by pretending to be indifferent. When she stopped coming (or stopped the regularity of these visits), I suffered her absence, had difficulty getting to sleep. My stance in this arrangement was to take no responsibility for what happened between us, but to acquiesce to erotic pleasure in the most grudging way.

And what did Cara Lou, my light sleeping wife, know? She must have heard something, thought something strange was going on? Did she suspect me of incest?

A month passed, six weeks in fact in this odd troublesome arrangement. I sometimes wondered if Valerie and Cara Lou were making it together when I wasn't around, though I believed (I felt an inexplicable surety about it) that it was not something they would do without me. We were all, in a sense certainly, married to one another, and I was the centerpiece of the arrangement. That was not my perception at the time. That was how Cara Lou saw us, or so she would reveal after things got out of hand later on.

One day at dinner (I had just gotten home from the theater), Valerie announced that she had gotten a job and a place to live and would be leaving us at the end of the week.

Cara Lou accepted the inevitable with her usual grace, seemed to fight back tears. "You could have stayed here," she said. "You know that you could have stayed, don't you?"

"You've been too generous to me, it's too much," Valerie said. "I've taken too much."

I was silent through all this, was trying to figure out what was really happening. Valerie's message, as it replayed itself in private echo, was that she was through with me (that was the part that weighed on me the most), and I felt rejected and sad. I should have also felt relieved, but I didn't and I couldn't figure out why. Wasn't trouble finally walking out the door? Trouble was going away, and I missed it with a sharp pang of loss in anticipation of its absence. What was that about?

I went to Valerie's room that night after I was sure, or thought, or hoped, that Cara Lou had gone to sleep.

She didn't seem particularly glad to see me—she was reading in bed when I came in—though didn't ask me to leave either. "I'm keeping my promise to you," she said, her face turned away. "I hope you're fucking pleased."

I tried to see the title of her book, but she put it down on the other side of her. The word "Housekeeping"caught my eye. "What promise is that?"

"How soon they forget. I gave you a promise that I would leave, and so I am. Leaving is what's happening, Jack."

"That was five months ago," I said. "I have no idea why you decided to come here, and I have even less idea why you decided, after all this time, to suddenly go away."

Her finger played along the back of my hand. "To tell you the truth, Jack, I imagined you were cheating me in some unfathomable way. I came here with the idea of making both of you sorry. So much for my intention. All I've succeeded in doing is making myself sad."

I had always been a sucker for a woman's confession, even when I had lingering doubts about its sincerity. I saw Valerie's intrusion in a new light, admired the riskiness of it. My domestic terrorist sweetheart, I thought. My heart opened to her.

We weren't quite making love, were playing with the inevitable as if it were only a conjecture (actually Valerie was lying on top of me), when Cara Lou lightly stepped into the room without bothering to knock.The room was dark so it was possible that we had already come apart by the time Cara Lou realized there was more than one of us. Valerie and I behaved with the exaggerated innocence of those who know themselves to be guilty. We presented ourselves as statues. Cara Lou said nothing at first, was breathing like the unseen stalker in a horror film.

Explanations offered themselves, one more unconvincing than the other, none spoken aloud. After a moment, Cara Lou joined us in the bed, moved under the covers and brought us all together in a crushing embrace. She melted us like some outpouring of liquid heat. It was, I confess, our best night together, one that filled me with exhilaration, and later the worst kind of depression.

The worst. I didn't get out of bed the next day, couldn't face Cara Lou, couldn't face myself. I had a performance that night, and I didn't have the presence of mind—the show must go on, right?—to call in sick. Before I went to the theater I packed my bags, but I left the house without them, would have forgotten myself if given the opportunity.

I hoped that performing would get me out of my funk, though I had no heart to go on stage. The first act I got through without any major gaffes, changing a few words here and there, improving on the text through lapses of memory. I was not so lucky in the second act, missing my first entrance, from which I never really recovered. "Sorry, I'm late," I ad-libbed when the stage manager woke me and pushed me on stage. The audience laughed.

The two actors on stage, Maria and Horst, had been killing time, improvising unconvincing conversation while desperately awaiting my arrival. My belated appearance seemed to bring the play, which had been in a coma in my absence, momentarily to life. I felt a rush of exhilaration, high on my own outrageousness, energy level never higher. I spoke my line to Maria, then stage whispered to the sparse crowd on the other side of the arch, "You ain't seen nothing yet," in the manner of some comic from my youth. The audience broke into applause. Though I was more or less the villain of the story, the unscrupulous interloper, I had become the hero of the moment.

I returned home after the performance (which lasted twenty minutes longer than usual, though otherwise pared down by omissions) in a considerably better mood than I left it. I no longer considered running off, though I had no idea of what I would say in defense of my deception.

Valerie is really just my half-sister, I thought of saying, but that would have muddied things even further.

The issue didn't come up. Cara Lou acted as if there had been no deception—everything as it had been,as it always was. She sat with me at dinner, kept me company as I ate, asked me about the events of my day.

"I got fired from the play," I said.

"There'll be others," she said. "Other plays, I mean."

Later, she asked me if I would come to her room—Valerie was conspicuously absent though not scheduled to leave us until the next morning—at about midnight. I said I would.

"You don't have to," she added.

"You don't have to read me my rights," I said. "Let's pretend I asked you first."

"I like pretense," she said, winking. "So we have a date, right?"

It was our usual routine, the main game of our marriage.

And yet I delayed going, sat in bed with my hands behind my head in some vaguely narcoleptic state. At one point in a rush of energy, I jumped out of bed as if it were on fire, though stopped myself at the door, returning in defeat to my original posture. What was I waiting for? It was already past midnight and I had to know Cara Lou would take my delay as a rejection. I was wondering what Valerie was doing, was thinking of Valerie. There had been no sound from her room, not even the ordinary turning from side to side, the slight snoring like breath catching against a thorn.

It was after two when the enchantment left me, and I made my way to Cara Lou's room. I knocked first and then went in without waiting for an invitation. She was asleep, seemed locked away on another planet, and I lay down next to her. She didn't wake, or even move in her sleep. Her breathing was barely perceptible, a distant hum. I nudged her with my knee. It took me awhile to register—too long—that this was not ordinary sleep. I spoke her name, whispered it, called her as if she were in another room. Then I turned on the light. The first thing I saw was an empty bottle of prescription pills on her end table alongside a folded note from her THANK YOU stationary. I shook her, pulled her up into a sitting position, slapped her face. "Uhh," she said, which meant she was still there.

I thought to get her into the shower, but I couldn't lift her, succeeded only in rolling her on to the floor. I went to her bathroom that adjoined the room, filled a glass of water, and poured it over her face. I had no presence of mind.

Valerie didn't come when I called her and I assumed—what else could I think?—that she was not there, that she had already gone on to something else.

I couldn't lift Cara Lou, so I rolled her across the rug toward the bathroom. "Bitch," I shouted at her. "Wake up."

"Cut out," she said.

"Get up, bitch," I said. "You're not getting away this easy." I got another glass of water and poured it on her. "Up," I ordered. "On your feet." She struggled to her knees, strangled on her breath and retched.

I got her into the bathroom, but still couldn't get her to her feet. I was afraid to leave her to call the hospital or to make a pot of coffee. "I don't want you to die," I said. "Listen to me. I don't want you to die. We're going to take a shower together." I got her under the armpits and lifted her up part way.

"No shower," she said. "Please."

It was at this point that Valerie came up behind me and said in a befogged voice, "All this shouting scares me."

"Call the hospital," I said, "and get an ambulance, will you?"

"I don't need an ambulance," Valerie said. "All I took was three pills."

Between us, we got Cara Lou to her feet and steadied her against a wall. Her eyes opened and shut like a doll's.

"Stay awake, baby," I said to her. "Awake," I shouted into her ear. "Who are you?"

"Nobody," she said.

Valerie called the hospital while I got Cara Lou to take a few steps. Without warning, we both collapsed under her weight. I was locked under her and couldn't breathe, could barely move.

An ambulance came after a while—it took them twenty minutes—and carted Cara Lou off in a stretcher. I helped them out the door with her and went along for the ride. Valerie came too.

She looked deathly by the time we got there, and Valerie and I sat in the reception room for the next five hours, awaiting word.

Valerie fell asleep in her chair while I paced. One time she opened her eyes sightlessly and whispered seemingly to no one, "I can't look at you."

Eventually word came from one of the nurses that she would make it, the worst had passed.

Cara Lou was returned from the hospital nine days later, alive, though changed in ways that I have difficulty defining.

First of all, she was thinner as if they had taken the air out of her. (Could she have lost fifty pounds in nine days or had she been losing weight all along?) And then there was the aura she had about her of hopelessness, of terminal disappointment.

When I visited her in the hospital, she begged me not to let them institutionalize her, which had been her doctor's recommendation. I promised that if it were in my power to stop them, I would. I held to my promise despite the doctor warning me that if she tried again and succeeded, her death would be on my head. "Do you want that kind of responsibility?" he asked.

"It won't happen again," I insisted. He shook his head in a superior way so many of them have and told me I was selfish and self-serving with this inappropriate smile on his face. I didn't defend myself, though the impulse was hard to resist.

The first thing she asked when she came home was, Where was Valerie? She looked through me as if I were glass or nothing at all. "Where is Valerie?"

I indicated with a shrug that I didn't care one way or another. "Are you all right?" I asked. She nodded. "I'm glad you're back and that you're all right."

"I've always known she's not your sister," Cara Lou said, not looking at me. "I knew that from the first day."

What was there to say? I went to my room to finish the packing I had started nine or ten days back in another lifetime. My shame defeated me. It was as if I had no fingers. I spent twenty minutes or so folding a single shirt, which persistently resisted me. When I was done I dragged my bags into the hallway and went to the closet to get my coat. There was no sign of Cara Lou, who had apparently closeted herself in her room.

"Goodbye," I said to no one. "I'm going." The doctor's smug warning that she would try again replayed itself in my head.

I heard or thought I heard (or wanted to hear), a ghostly voice, Cara Lou's voice calling, "Don't. Don't go."

"What?"

I waited a minute or so and the plea, if it ever was, was not repeated. I didn't want to stay; I only wanted to be forgiven. Then I thought, I can't leave someone alone who had just attempted suicide. There was no one else around (a nurse who was supposed to report hadn't shown up), so I called Cara Lou's sister, who I knew didn't work, and asked her to come over. "Cara Lou shouldn't be left alone," I said.

"What about you," the sister said in her argumentative voice. "Why aren't you staying with her? Isn't that what you're paid for?"

I didn't take the bait. "We're splitting up," I said. "She doesn't want me here. I'll wait until you get here before I go."

"I have no intention of being Cara Lou's baby sitter," she said and hung up. So then I called Valerie.

She said no, she couldn't, wouldn't come, didn't ever want to see either of us again, but she showed up almost immediately after hanging up on me.

We were a sorry bunch. Cara Lou embraced Valerie at the door. While the two women hugged, I watched jealously. Then I joined them, found myself between them, arms around them both. "My two people," Cara Lou said. "We are a marriage together."

"What does that mean, a marriage together?" I asked her.

"It means you don't have to leave," she whispered to me as if it were a secret that excluded Valerie, who was standing next to us. "A wife forgives a husband everything."

I felt unforgiven and unforgiving, unworthy of forgiveness, though I considered continuing our bizarre life together out of a kind of inertia. Valerie carried my bags to my room. "If you want me here, I'll stay," I said. Cara Lou clapped her hands. I felt defeated.

The old routine continued in its self-mocking way for another week, another two weeks.

There was a night I went to Cara Lou's room—it was something like five in the morning—and discovered Valerie in bed with her, both women asleep. I didn't wake them, returned to my assigned room in a state of dislocation.

And though I agreed to stay—I had been happy in that house for some of the time—I took off when an opportunity presented itself. (The women had been out for several hours, shopping at Bloomingdale's for fall outfits.) There were too many bad feelings in the air between us, too much shame, too much that couldn't be forgiven. Besides, I told myself, they had each other. I was unnecessary. I had no future in that house and not much present (or presence) either. That marriage was over.

As far away as I got from them—I went to Los Angeles—it never seemed far enough. When I sent my address I received signed divorce papers in the mail with an accompanying note and a certified check for six figures that I kept in a drawer for years.

"I won't forget you," the note said. "Valerie sends her love though she refuses to admit it." It was signed, "Your former wife, Cara Lou."

I knew how to start things and end things, but not what

to do in between.

Having failed at marriage five times running, I nevertheless felt I was beginning to get the knack of it, and if another chance came my way, I was confident that this time I would get it right.

6
The Two Most Beautiful Women

I stayed single for several years after that, not looking for trouble or not looking for the same trouble I had had five times over in the past. What I was looking for (in fact, I was hardly looking at all) was something new, something qualitatively different from any of my previous adventures in the relationship trade. What I imagined myself to want was a woman without the self-doubts and insecurities that had caused most of my other marriages to come to grief.

This was my reasoning. A beautiful woman, given the

values of the culture, would have less to prove than someone marginally attractive or someone, as in Cara Lou's case, so vastly overweight as to seem socially unacceptable. The more beautiful, I thought, the less reason to be vulnerable. At the same time, I was wary of the dangers of narcissism. I wanted a woman so thoroughly beautiful, so secure in her sense of being beautiful, that the impression her beauty made on others had ceased to interest her.

An ideal is never easy to find, but the pursuit of it of course has its own interest. During this period, between my fifth and sixth wife, I dated only women who were (in my eyes) surpassingly beautiful.

In my quest for the right woman, the perfect one, I met with a series of disappointments. I was a producer in Hollywood at the time and so I had access to some (all, I sometimes thought) of the most beautiful women in the English speaking world. As a matter of scruple, I did not use my position to woo these women.

I'd like to describe the nature of my disappointments, some of them. We're talking about a period of seven years here. Between the ages of twenty-one and thirty-eight, I had been married five times. The longest period between marriages had been eighteen months, and that was after the breakup of my first. When I married for the first time, I assumed in my unjaded innocence it was forever.

So this was a period in which I was (while in pursuit of an elusive ideal) learning to be alone. I made it a point not to have a woman sleep over—at least not the same woman, I was on a quest—more than four nights a week. I studied privacy as if it were advanced calculus.

The disappointments were small, but continuous. Beautiful women, I kept discovering, the ones that crossed my path, had no more self-confidence than more ordinary women. Take Sarah Hubb, for example.

Sarah Hubb was not an actress or a model but a writer and film editor, and the most interesting beautiful woman I had met in Hollywood up to that point.

She was prematurely white-haired.

She was not really what I was looking for, not at all (never) what I had in mind.

I fell in love with her on second or third sight, fell in love with the idea of her as opposed to an idea of something else.

She didn't like me at first, not much, not for the longest time. That was a liability. It wasn't that exactly either, the not liking, the insistent, out-front disapproval. It was that she didn't take me seriously, didn't believe when I said I loved her that I never lied about matters of the heart.

Why didn't she believe me?

"You talked of love to too many other women," she said. "Words overused lose their meaning."

Yes. Yes. Yes. Still, I thought it had to do with feelings about herself, her prematurely white hair, her small breasts.

I never believed it had to do with me. The more I protested my love to her, the cooler she became to me. We had the same conversation, variations on it, on several occasions. She suggested that we end our affair (and why did she need my consent?), and I presented arguments for continuing things as they were.

And each time she relented, agreed to continue as if

continuing were a matter of no choice, an aspect of defeat.

She had a history of falling in love with stormtroopers, wife beaters, emotional torturers, marginal sociopaths. She was attracted to men, she said, who had no doubts.

One day at a party on the yacht of a man who was considered the hottest of the new breed of producer/directors, I saw the most beautiful woman in the world standing between my host and his current wife. Her beauty, the intensity of it, scared me. I couldn't look at her and I couldn't look away.

I kept track of her, knew at almost every moment where she was, who she was talking to or standing next to, without going up to her or seeking an introduction. My opportunity would come. It was a smallish party in a small space. If I didn't move, she would eventually find her way to me. A woman that beautiful, I thought, would have a natural resistance to being pursued.

I was prepared to be disappointed when we finally met.

Her name was Nadia, and she spoke English with one of those accents that American actors used to use when playing immigrants or characters in foreign countries. She was almost as charming as she was beautiful.

"What do you do?" I asked her.

"I don't do," she said. "I merely am." She laughed at the pretentiousness of her remark, mocked herself.

"Are you an actress?"

"I'm a guest," she said. "A guest, from where I come, is also an actress."

That was the extent of our conversation during our first encounter. I omit something. "I'd like to fuck you," I said to her. It was what I said to attractive women that year. I was into direct expression of feeling.

It took a moment for her to react. She raised her eyebrows in a mild display of outrage and walked away. Perhaps it was the wrong thing to say to her.

The only thing to do was to apologize, and I waited a suitable time—twenty minutes exactly—before going after her. She was talking to Lucretia Oldwyn, the wife of the man who owned the yacht, and I approached on the pretense of paying respects to my hostess.

That done (Lucretia presented her cheek to be kissed as if it were the pope's ring), there was the inevitable introduction. I held out my hand to Nadia, waited for her to say we had already met, which she didn't. She shook my hand as if we were meeting for the first time.

When Lucretia moved on, Nadia said to me, "You're persistent, aren't you, Mr. Cole?"

Her beauty overwhelmed me, deprived me of speech. I searched her astonishing face for a flaw. "I want to apologize for my crudeness," I mumbled.

"It's forgotten," she said, turning away and then returning to stare at my face as I had hers. She had more poise than almost anyone I had ever met, woman or man. Yet there was something vulnerable about her too, something invisibly and mysteriously vulnerable, which made me admire her all the more.

I thought of saying, You're the most beautiful woman I've ever seen, but I didn't. I didn't want to emphasize what I thought of as her advantage. Instead I said, "I like the way you look."

She half-smiled at my ungenerous compliment. "You intrigue me," she said with her intriguing though undefined accent.

I gave her my card. "You ever take a screen test, Nadia? I'd like to put you in front of the camera."

She fingered my card, studied it, then turned it over as if a more interesting message might be hidden on the reverse side, then handed it back. "I'm afraid not for me," she said, reproducing her dazzling smile as if she were on camera.

And why didn't I believe her? She assumed the worst, I imagined, had every reason to assume the worst. And I compounded the misunderstanding by denying what on the surface of things seemed undeniable. "My offer of a screen test was not a bribe to get you to sleep with me," I said. "That's not the way I do things."

She waved off my objection as if to say it's unnecessary to defend yourself to me who is not interested enough to make such judgments about you. A moment or so later, she found her excuse to move away.

Later, much later, I saw a screen test she had taken for the man who had given the party on his yacht, and I was surprised at how lifeless she seemed. The camera frightened her, and she hid from it by denying herself.

At about the same time, or perhaps a week or so earlier, I saw her in her first film in which she played a courtesan (of sorts) in ancient Egypt with one eyebrow raised and her odd French-Romanian accent and no other conviction whatsoever. I was her lover at the time and escorted her to the screening. She had not the slightest idea how bad she was, couldn't understand the audience's ironic laughter at her most serious moments. To console her, I said I would put her in a movie in which her great charm and luminous beauty would shine through whatever role she played. I gave her my word, something I don't do lightly, that I would make a star out of her. It was then I arranged to see her impossible screen test.

She was a stunningly beautiful woman for whom the camera had no love. It turned her to stone with a glance. Her screen test was an inescapable prophesy of the zombielike performance she gave in her first film.

I had made her a promise, and I had a reputation I dined on for not welshing on my word. Not everyone liked me, but even my biggest detractors knew when I said I would do something it was going to happen. I was bound and determined to make Nadia a star—not an actress, there was little hope there—but an unforgettable presence on the screen, a charismatic personality like Garbo or Dietrich. The trick was to have the camera fall in love with her before she had opportunity to resist its adoration. The camera could make no demands, must be humble and unassuming, must worship her and desire her without hope of reward; we're talking zen hard-on here, something passionate, delicate, and desireless.

I was too full of myself to accept the possibility that I couldn't do what couldn't be done, believed in those days I could do virtually anything. How difficult could it be to make Nadia as goddesslike on screen as she was in person? All I wanted was an illusion that stood up to the real.

She was never really interested in my plans for her,

had a different set of aspirations, or no aspirations at all.

I made lists of directors and cameramen who were good with women. I screened their films night after night in my basement, studied them frame by frame, sometimes alone, sometimes with the dozing Nadia at my side. Her apparent indifference to my quest drove me wild.

In the meantime, the most beautiful woman in the world lived with me, shared my bed, which gave me a euphoric sense of unearned triumph. Also, she was exciting in bed, particularly in the beginning of our relationship when we were a secret item. It wasn't that she was passionate but that she knew how to please, offered continuous variety.

I haven't mentioned how we got together, how I took her away from H. K. Oldwyn. I haven't mentioned it because there's really little to say that does me credit. I wore her down; I pursued her as if she were the most important thing in my life. And at some point Oldwyn tired of her—I suspect his wife insisted he break it off—and sent Nadia away. The chronology has its gray areas. Perhaps she had already become my lover before H.K. Oldwyn, that tired enfant terrible, was disposed to give her up.

It's possible that Lucretia found out her husband was sleeping with Nadia and demanded that H.K. choose between them. That was what Sarah Hubb told me, though how she knew I had no idea.

When I told Sarah Hubb that I would probably end up

marrying Nadia, she said she would marry me herself to save me from such a disastrous liaison. That's when she told me about Lucretia forcing her husband to throw Nadia out. Two-thirds of Oldwyn's holdings were in Lucretia's name.

In Nadia's version, she had been the one to break with Oldwyn. "The man had what you would call unacceptable needs," she said in her charming accent. "All I want was to be his good friend. What he want was totally humiliating to me."

Obsessed with fulfilling my promise to Nadia, I spent six months staring at her with a movie camera, put her through the ordeal of at least a half dozen screen tests, using different cameramen and different equipment before even concerning myself with a script. She had astonishing purple eyes, but in one of the tests in which the background was a similar velvety purple, it looked as if you could see right through her head.

When Nadia moved out of H.K. Oldwyn's guest house, she moved—it was to be a temporary arrangement—into mine. As a matter of fact, I had no guest house. I offered what I had to offer, a room in my house, which turned out to be the one I slept in. That wasn't my intention: to have her move in with me, to have her move into my bed.

I had wooed her so relentlessly, she assumed, or appeared to assume, that I would do anything for her. "I'm going to have to move in with you for awhile," she said. "I hope that's not inconvenient."

"My pleasure," I said. "My house is yours for as long as you want to stay."

"I knew you want me to live with you." she said. "You've been after me to be with you since we met. Now you get your way, okay?" It was her stance to take nothing from anyone, even of course when the evidence said otherwise. She made a point of retaining the illusion of her independence.

Even though she was the most beautiful woman I had ever seen, I began by invisible degrees to tire of Nadia, though I didn't allow myself to assimilate that knowledge until she had gone. (As sexy as she was, she tended to efface herself in lovemaking, as she did before the eye of the camera.) Tire is perhaps the wrong word for what I felt. Or that it was myself I tired of and not Nadia. Nadia was never less than advertised. She wasn't unintelligent or without imagination or without traces of a sense of humor. She merely in some essential way wasn't there much of the time. And I never tired of looking at her astonishing face.

For a stunningly beautiful woman she had no vanity. It irritated her to be stared at and since I couldn't not look (she was my obsession), I had to observe her on the sly, a voyeur, in a sense, in my own house. Perhaps her most interesting quality was the unexpectedness of her charmingly eccentric European accent.

So I developed this movie project for Nadia about a goddess who comes down to earth to find out what it's like to love a mortal. Our story.

A week into the shooting of the picture, which was

called *Heaven on Earth,* she complained to me (in bed) that she couldn't work with the director, a benign tyrant with a gifted eye, a man I had chosen for the elegance of his frames. He didn't know how to talk to people, she purred in my ear; he shouted too much; he insulted her intelligence.

I said I would take care of it, though did nothing (I never liked being manipulated), assuming the problem would take care of itself. The situation worsened. Nadia reiterated her demands with greater and greater passion. The man was a brute, she said, a thug, a gangster of cruelty, he could not be tolerated a moment longer. If he continued as director, she would have no choice but to leave the film.

I said I would talk to the director, whom I knew to be a reasonable man, no more autocratic than the general run, but Nadia insisted the problem between them was beyond reconciliation.

As chance would have it, the next day I got a note from the director asking for a meeting. His complaint, it turned out, was similar to Nadia's, though from an opposing standpoint. The woman was impossible, he said, was untalented, did not take direction. He could not work with her. So of course I had to replace him. What else was there to do?

The problems didn't end. The second director, who was a cut less distinguished than the first, who had a reputation as a woman's director, got along with Nadia from the word go, managed her by making love to her, handled her by handling her. Of course I didn't know that at the time. The dailies I saw were banal but serviceable. Nadia, however, looked beautiful—almost as beautiful as she did in real life—and that for the time being seemed sufficient. I brought in another writer, a novelist with two screen credits and a drinking problem, to enliven the script.

We saw so little of each other—I had to be on location in Mexico for awhile with another project—our relationship seemed to move in reverse. We grew estranged before we had arrived at intimacy. Sometimes she looked at me when I came through the door of my own house after a few days absence as if I were a potentially dangerous intruder.

"I didn't expect you back so soon," she said one time when I arrived unexpectedly. Something in her voice made me want to open all the closets or look under the bed.

I looked for flaws in her beauty, sought disillusionment. Only in certain light was such scrutiny rewarded.

I had won the most beautiful woman in the world and didn't know what to do with her now that I had her. Though we talked of a future together, we shared no intimacy beyond our willed sexual games. She might have been Miss Mars (what a title for a film!) for all I understood of her. Something, some part of her—her soul, for God's sake—was always held back. Was that the attraction? Her elegant opacity? I loved her the way a camera loves certain faces. She was the perfect image of female beauty on my internalized movie screen.

We didn't hold conversations so much as report our adventures to each other while apart. Her stories were almost always unconvincing and rarely if ever interesting in themselves. They nevertheless had the considerable charm of ingenuous lies told unaffectedly by a beautiful woman. Sometimes I watched her tell the stories rather than listen to the words. Her flawless face was her undeniable authority.

Having her with me was like having an exquisite object on display. I still liked looking at her particularly while making love, which she tolerated with bemused indifference, but after a while everything else seemed beside the point. Even our sex life began to run downhill. Her lack of pleasure in our various sexual games undermined my own. She seemed to have zero sense of herself beyond physical image. She loved to be admired but not stared at, afraid that staring would uncover some aspect of herself she needed to keep secret.

When she announced in bed that she had decided to get her own place, I said, "Why don't you marry me instead?" That had been on my mind for a while, the idea of asking her to marry me. She seemed less surprised to receive the offer than I had felt in hearing myself make it. "I didn't know people like us got married in this time," she said. That was the only answer she gave me.

The picture I was producing with her (and for her), *Heaven on Earth*, despite my having to replace the director and (twice) the male lead, was near wrap-up. Almost all of the principal shooting had been completed.

I had the fantasy that after the movie was released (and our respective careers advanced), we would wrap up our life together by getting married. The film, in a certain sense (allow me this), was our wedding gift to one another. If I wasn't in love with Nadia, not wholly, not irreversibly, I nevertheless doted on the movie of us together I carried around in my head.

Sarah Hubb was the cutter for *Heaven on Earth* and that of course—I see this now in retrospect—had to be asking for trouble. I didn't know then that Sarah Hubb cared enough for me to be jealous of Nadia. The movie opened and closed in the same week and was the source of amusement to a number of reviewers. Everyone panned the film except one avant-garde magazine that saw it as a "savagely satirical commentary on the medium itself." In this review/article, which came out a month or two after the film's demise, Nadia was singled out as one of "the great absurdist figures in the post-modern cinema." Nadia, as it happened, was not in the country when her single favorable notice appeared.

In most of the negative reviews, Nadia was the chief source of the critics' malicious fun, which was more of a surprise to her than the painful disappointment it might have been. "I don't think I'm so bad," she said to me. "Do you think I'm so bad as they say?"

What could I tell her? That we had just collaborated on what may have been the worst film of the decade on a budget of over twenty million. "They missed the point," I said, which was a partial truth. We all missed the point. After *Heaven on Earth*, my judgment was suspect. I was no longer bankable.

"They did," she said, "didn't they? I was supposed to be figure of comic dimension. The real joke is on them, though the picture was not at all perfect."

"It didn't conform to the general expectation," I said.

She was in her room packing her two suitcases. I watched her without saying anything.

"I think I go to Paris until the dust settles," she said.

"When I get back if you still want, if we both still want, maybe we tie the knot, yes?"

A car came to the door to take her to the airport—I offered to drive her myself but she wouldn't have it—and we shook hands at the door with the formality of business associates dissolving a partnership. I had failed to deliver on my promise, and she would not forgive me.

And so the most beautiful woman in the world left me never, I had to believe, to return. She was wearing a short black raincoat and a red hat, which is how I would remember her, when she climbed into the back seat of the limousine. She waved from the car as if she was dismissing a servant, and as I turned my head away, she disappeared into the future.

That was not the end of her in my life, only the presumed end.

Five months later I received a letter from Nadia (postmarked Romania), announcing that she was returning to the States in ten days. That wasn't the whole message. She was ready, she wrote, "to be the loving wife you had been all your life in looking for."

The letter could not have arrived at a more unpropitious moment. Sarah Hubb had just moved in with me, and we were talking—I was talking—about us getting married. I had assumed that Nadia was out of the picture. Sarah was saying, "I'd have to be crazy to marry you" more often now so I had to believe that her resistance to the prospect was diminishing.

When I showed Sarah Nadia's letter, she said (we had been talking about something else, about who had played the male lead in the movie, *Dark Corridor*), "If I were you, I'd call my lawyer." Then she said, moving her hand through her white hair, "If you really want to marry this Romanian gold digger, I'll pack my bags and take off. This lady has no plans to make trouble for you."

"And you think the other lady has?"

"I think the other lady wants to marry you. She says so, doesn't she? She says you proposed to her and she's accepting. You did propose to her, didn't you?"

"That was a long time ago," I said. "A proposal doesn't mean forever."

"Talk to your lawyer," said Sarah Hubb, who came from a family of lawyers and knew how dangerous they could be to the unwary.

I didn't talk to a lawyer, not then, procrastinated on what to do about Nadia, ended up writing her a letter (which said very little) to an address which I had no certainty would reach her. My intention was to delay her return until I was clear as to what I wanted.

Two weeks later—it seemed like the next day—Nadia and her steamer trunk arrived on my doorstep. It was past midnight, perhaps several hours past. Sarah Hubb had already gone to bed for the night, and I was watching a movie on video tape. I tended to fall asleep more readily in front of the television set than anywhere else. So her arrival—I wasn't quite sure where I was as I got up to answer the door—had the aspect of a dream or a dream within a dream.

"It was no good to leave," were her first words, her accent heavier than I remembered it.

"Did you get my letter?" I asked.

She looked ruefully at me. "You never write," she said. "You never write a word."

"I sent you a letter," I said, "telling you that I had not

expected you to return and that I was living with someone else."

My beautiful guest looked heavenward, which in this case was at a light fixture in my vestibule. "Yes," she whispered. "The letter was sent nowhere and to nowhere it arrive safely."

"I sent it to the address you left me," I said.

Her eyes filled with tears—the first time I had seen her cry not on screen, not in performance. "All my money is spent in getting here. You need to let me stay. Nothing else I ask for, nothing."

How could I refuse such a request? I said I would stake her to a hotel room for two weeks, would drive her to one first thing in the morning, after we all had a good night's sleep.

Nadia stayed around for a while, finding new excuses each day not to leave, playing havoc with my life. After three days of her unwanted presence, she no longer seemed the most beautiful woman I had ever seen. I began to discover flaws in her face I had never even imagined before. Her astonishing purple eyes were too close together, were getting closer as the days passed, she had a small pimple on her chin, lines of discontent at the corners of her mouth. Her flaws mocked my initial judgment of her. I could no longer look at her (though there were moments I confess when it was as it was) with unequivocal pleasure.

My willed disappointment, I suspect, released me from her thrall.

It was not that Sarah Hubb was any more impatient than I was with Nadia's uninvited presence. It was just that she didn't trust that I preferred her to Nadia, and the more I insisted on it, the less she wanted to believe me.

I had to do something to keep her so I did what I had done so many times before; I proposed marriage, proposed that we marry as soon as possible. I had married once before in California, so I knew something about the licensing laws.

"Yes, of course," Sarah said. "Yes. But not while that woman's living with us."

"She's promised to leave in a few days," I said. "The only way to get her to leave against her will is to call the police, and I don't want to do that. If we got married, Sarah, it would speed her along."

"I don't want to talk about it," she said, the blood rushing to her cheeks from some invisible slap. "The subject depresses me."

There was no warning or announcement in advance. One afternoon at about two o'clock, a taxi appeared at my door, and Nadia boarded without a word and was gone.

The day after that, Sarah and I got our licenses, and two days after that—perhaps it was even the next day—we got married at the house of friends. That was how I got married for the sixth time after vowing I would marry the most beautiful woman in the world or never marry again. At the conclusion of the ceremony, when I turned to kiss her, I thought, Yes I have just married the most beautiful woman in the world.

We had a six day honeymoon in Paris, which I will talk about later, then returned to my house to live and to resume our respective work.

We had a surprise in store for us, the one that Sarah had anticipated.

How I found out is less important than what it was. I was being sued by Nadia (and her high-priced lawyer) for "breach of promise," and something called "sexual malfeasance." The asking price was twenty thousand a month palimony. I didn't take it seriously, thought I could clear it up directly with Nadia without having to deal with her killer lawyer.

The problem was, I had no way of reaching Nadia, no forwarding address, no names of friends who might know where she was. I asked around, even called her lawyer, but got nowhere.

It was three ten in the morning, and I had been unable to sleep—the business, you see, had upset me—so I went into her room. I went through the drawers of her dresser, I looked under her bed, I looked in her bed. She had been thorough or perhaps had never unpacked. The only thing she had left behind were a stack of publicity photos, 5 by 7's. They were machine-signed, Love always, Nadia.

Eventually I found her, ran her down. Although I'm thought of as an outsider in this town, there are some people around willing to do me a favor for a price. She was living in a small Malibu hotel, her rent (I learned this later) paid for by the married lawyer who had taken her case. I went to see her, bribed my way past the desk clerk and went directly to her room unannounced.

At first she wouldn't let me in, said she hated me. When she opened the door, when she finally opened the door, it was a shock to see her. "Don't look," she said. "I'm not myself." Her hair was scraggly, unwashed, her face swollen out of shape. She was virtually unrecognizable.

"What the hell happened to you?"

"Nothing. I have fucking allergic reaction. Don't look at me. I want to say you are the most selfish man I ever know."

"Is that why your lawyer's suing me?"

"Yes. Not at all. You should leave. I'm not to talk to you."

"Your lawyer told you not to talk to me. That's it, isn't it? He's afraid if you talk to me, you'll change your mind."

"Please to leave." She pointed a melodramatic finger toward the door, an unconvincing actress even in real life.

"Are you on something, Nadia? What's wrong with you?" She was stumbling, and I held on to her.

"What's wrong with you?" she said, mimicking me. Then she began to scream. I tightened my hold on her and eventually—the screaming went on for a long time; it was a tantrum she was having—she quieted, fell into an almost catatonic silence, as if all the noise in her had leaked out.

"You were the most beautiful woman I ever saw," I said. "The most beautiful."

"You liar," she said under her breath.

"The most beautiful woman anyone ever saw."

She pushed me away, and I released her, and she went around the unmade bed and sat with her back to me. "You shouldn't say that to me. You have no right to say such things to me. I don't listen. You are a devil." She put her hands over her ears.

"Why do you think you have a right to my money? Whose idea is this?"

"What?"

I repeated the question in a considerably louder voice, and I got the same unacknowledgement, the same infuriating, "What?" Then she muttered something behind her hand.

I moved toward her. "Talk to me, Nadia," I said.

"I'm your wife," she said. "I give you my best years. You use me up."

"Is that what your lawyer told you to say? Nadia, you only lived with me for eight months."

"I'll tell you something," she whispered, as if someone who mattered might overhear. "I really hate you. Really. Really. Really."

This was the most deeply felt thing she had said to me in all the time I knew her. I felt obliged to acknowledge what I felt was going on between us. That's why I did what I did. It may have been the only thing I could do. The pushing her against the wall, that was for love, for what she had meant to me, for what had never been said. The responsibility is mine. I fucked her against the wall. She was no longer breathtakingly beautiful but she was there this time, she felt something, she bit and scratched, bruised my neck with a venomous kiss, she tilted on the edge of pleasure. It felt to me like an obligation, a concluding gesture. Then I went home to my wife, to Sarah Hubb.

She knew where I had been and knew what I had done, which is to say I confessed the worst. And she didn't forgive me, would not forgive me, not ever.

It was as if I had made the wrong choice twice.

And as Sarah pulled away from me, drew further into herself—women have that secret place—she seemed unbearably beautiful.

I made periodic efforts to erase the damage, apologized, refused to apologize, insisted that I had done nothing wrong, pleaded for her to relent and forgive me. In the short run, each of my strategies, whichever, had some positive effect. "It's over," Sarah would insist, or "It's forgiven." Or: "I don't blame you, Jack." But nothing changed.

We lived together like strangers in a death camp for another six months. Much of that time I spent trying to ingratiate myself to Sarah Hubb. Someone had to keep the marriage going, and I was the only one to whom it seemed to matter. Whenever she admired something or seemed to—a necklace, a painting, a silk scarf, a pair of shoes—I contrived to make her a gift of it. She received my gifts like mail sent to the wrong address.

I whispered to her in bed one night, "I chose to marry you."

She sighed in her half sleep as if my voice were an intrusion on some better dream.

I continued to pursue her favor, worked at it relentlessly, determined to keep this marriage from failing. I thought of this, my sixth marriage, as my last shot.

How did it seem to her, this persistent ineffectual wooing,this unencouraged pursuit? I imagined the worst: contempt and a kind of horror.

I thought about what was going on between us, how foolish it must have seemed, and I thought, well why don't I try something else. The thing is, I couldn't think of anything else to try.

I said to her over dinner, "If you don't want to live with me, why don't you move out?"

"I'll move out if you want me to," she said.

I didn't understand her response. "If you're going to be my enemy, I'd like you to move out," I said.

She looked at me, her eyes narrowed, a last reading of the text. "No problem," she said.

We were polite to each other for the rest of the meal, as if we both regretted what we had allowed ourselves to say.

Whatever had been decided seemed irreversible. Shortly after dinner, Sarah went into our bedroom to pack. I knew what she was doing, and I didn't want her to go, but I made no effort to dissuade her. I made no effort because I assumed that nothing I might say would change her mind.

Someone rang the bell just as she completed packing, and I was the one to answer the door. I called to her, "Sarah, it's for you."

"Just a minute," she called back.

The friend who had come for her—I knew him slightly; he was someone she worked with—waited for her in the doorway. "She'll be a minute," I said.

He waited for her by looking the other way, staring off into some unpopulated distance. Her delay seemed interminable.

When she emerged, she kept her head averted, said nothing, not even goodbye, and it was only after she was gone that I realized—she was wearing an uncharacteristic excess of makeup—that she had been trying to disguise the fact that she had been crying.

It meant nothing; her tears meant nothing. I closed

the door, though I don't remember closing it, and I walked through the house, visiting in turn each of its twelve rooms. Sarah Hubb was in none of them. I had the sense that I was missing something obvious, that Sarah's apparent absence was a manifestation of my forgetfulness. I had misplaced my wife, who was 5' 7" tall and weighed 110 pounds, in this oversized house. There was loneliness in every room.

It was not that I didn't understand what had happened with Sarah Hubb. What I didn't understand was something else, how it had happened, how I had let it happen. I had no language to know what it was that I didn't know.

And why, given my contrition, had she been unable to forgive me? Had I behaved so badly? Isn't everything at some point forgivable?

I saw her at work from time to time—she was editing a film I was connected with—and for a week or so we avoided each other, and then we began to fall into our old banter, the way it was when we were first friends.

We pretended, or seemed to pretend, that this was the way it had always been, that nothing had intervened—not living together, not marriage, not betrayal and disaffection.

For no reason, or some reason—there is always some reason—I found myself thinking about my honeymoon with Sarah Hubb, focusing on one incident in particular.

We had been shy with each other on our token honeymoon in Paris, inexplicably distant and diffident. A certain wariness had developed between us without recognizable cause. Leaving a restaurant after dinner, we got into a mild argument about whether we ought to walk back to our hotel or take the metro. I urged walking. Sarah Hubb pretended not to care, acquiesced to my insistence. We walked a block or two in silence, then she said in an uncharacteristically harsh voice: "You don't love me. You shouldn't have married me."

I said something like, "What do you mean? Of course I love you."

Her remark was not repeated. She leaned toward me, and we kissed. She swayed when I held her, seemed by turns frail or fierce, some twig in the wind or the wind itself. We were in the middle of the street, several blocks from our hotel, cleaving to the same space.

"Let's find a cab," I think I said.

Her grip became tighter. "Five minutes," she pleaded. I didn't understand what she wanted. People stared at us as if we were some form of street theater. "It's silly to do this in the street," I said or tried to say. Her mouth seemed to swallow my words, steal them before they were spoken.

Her abandon in this public place, which was uncharacteristic (Sarah tended to be shy in public), fueled a kind of anxiety. A cab was coming, and I signaled to it, but it went by without acknowledgment.

"I don't want to be anywhere else," she whispered. "Do you?"

The question was asked as if it had only one answer. I said, "What I want is to be alone with you, only that."

It was a damp night and seemed to be getting wetter, a serious storm in imminent promise. That was my recollection. It may have been that I confused the weather with my feelings.

Eventually, we disentangled, and I found a taxi, and we went back to our hotel room. We took off our clothes in a rush of activity, but didn't touch for the longest time, stood naked a foot or two apart looking at each other in exquisite anticipation. Sarah seemed to be shivering from the cold, though our room was if anything hotter than ideal. I was in a fever, my face burning. I didn't want to begin, even to move toward the prospect of beginning, because to begin meant ultimately to end. The idea of ending, you have to understand, was unbearable to me. Finally I held out my hand to her, which she ignored at first, then held on to loosely with two hands as if it were a damaged bird, something inordinately fragile. So much tremulousness and hesitation over doing something we had done a hundred times before. What was that about? We met under the covers, entering the bed from opposing sides.

There was a shocking intensity of feeling between us that night, an intensity that threatened to make anticlimax of the next day or the next week or the next twenty years. It left us nowhere to go. "My life," she whispered to me. "You're wonderful," I think I said in return. That may have been all that was said. They were insufficient acknowledgements of what had passed. Not lies, but impassioned evasions.

In the morning, I was burned out and frightened. Whatever it was that possessed me that night, I knew I had to avoid its recurrence to survive. So I turned off, sought calmer air. Later, when I became aware that that intensity of feeling was gone forever from my life, I secretly mourned its loss while pretending to be unconcerned. What else could I do, what else could I possibly do?

My sense is that that night in Paris represented the high and low points of our marriage, love and heartbreak, which were the same, love and love's loss. The rest was terminal disappointment.

I let myself believe—I never wholly believed otherwise—that Sarah Hubb never loved me. Never. Everything else between us was read in light of that assumption. She didn't love me, never loved me. Her gestures to the contrary didn't mean what they seemed.

So I lost her. If I ever wished to undo anything, I might have wished unwritten that last scene with Sarah Hubb the night she left (the day I asked her to leave) forever. Yet I suspect even if I had not asked her to leave, even if I had found the words to make possible reconciliation, the outcome would have been more or less the same. We were not getting along. Eventually, if not then, a month later or a year or five years down the road, we would have found our way apart. It's my rule of thumb not to look back. I rarely have regrets, and I never, not even to myself, admit to having them.

7
The Last Resembles the First

After the breakup of my marriage to Sarah Hubb, which was my sixth, I went through an extended period of withdrawal and depression, cut myself off from long time friends, watched myself age in fast forward. My heart was young. It kept itself secret, hidden as it was in an aging unkempt body—my pretender self, my surrogate, my scruffy disguise. I didn't jog or swim or work out or play tennis or watch my diet, did few or none of the things my generation was doing to court the illusion of defeating time. I looked ancient in the harsh eye of the mirror, was trapped in some old man's earthly clothes. I could have been my father, who died on my birthday twenty years ago. My reflection recalled his last face.

I was in Provincetown Massachusetts, a guest in the house of recent friends, people I barely knew (well, that's another story), when I saw this attractive woman on the beach who bore my first wife, Regina, an astonishing resemblance. Time collapsed for me, and I called to her, called her Regina, forgetting for the moment that Regina would be my age now and this woman was little more than half of that.

The odd thing was the woman raised her head at my call, looked at me with some hint of recognition before she spoke. "I'm not who you think," she called back, as if she too had her doubts.

Who was she if she wasn't R? That question would occupy me in a variety of ways for a long time.

"You look like someone I used to know," I said.

"How interesting," she said. "You look like someone I would have liked to have known." She gave me barely a glance before she was on her way along the water's edge, a man I hadn't noticed before trailing deferentially a half step behind.

The resemblance to Regina, or at least to my memory of Regina, was so strong I found it difficult to believe this woman could be anyone else. It was possible—the idea hit me in the middle of the night, the residue of a dream—that Regina had a much younger sister. She would have had to have been conceived, however, after R and I had separated. The Regina I knew had been an only child.

I returned to the same Truro beach at the same time the next day hoping to see her again. For several days I kept vigil, haunted the spot of our first meeting without reward. My hosts, who were with me at that first chance meeting, said they might have seen the woman somewhere before, but they were sure she wasn't a Provincetown person. My host, Oscar, who was a therapist, lectured me on the dangers of obsessive behavior.

Twice I thought I saw her from a distance, only to discover on coming closer (exhilaration dying) that it was someone else, someone who bore her virtually no resemblance.

I drove up and down the cape in a rented Dodge Polaris, playing out some hopeless scenario.

Circumstance took me to the Now Voyager Motel on the outskirts of East Sandwich. Accident served me, blind luck. She was coming out of the local pharmacy as I ambled by on my melancholy way to nowhere in particular.

"Well, hello," she said, and the odd thing was I didn't recognize her right away. "We met a few weeks ago on that beautiful Truro Beach," she told me. "You said, if you remember, that I reminded you of someone you had been close to a long time ago."

I took the advantage she offered me, didn't let on that I remembered her. She was wearing a black dress which, though short-skirted, seemed inappropriate for summer. It was hard to pinpoint the change in her. She seemed to be wearing more or less makeup, to have either gained or lost weight, to have restyled her hair or changed the shape of her nose. I didn't want to seem to be staring at her.

She shrugged at my perplexity. "Hey, I would have known you anywhere," she said. "You look even more like yourself than the last time."

"How do you mean, more like myself?"

"It was just an observation," she said. "Nothing worth analyzing. Well, I have to get going."

"I'll walk along with you," I said. Though the resemblance to Regina seemed less remarkable this time, she nevertheless reminded me of someone (unnamed, unnameable) I had known in the distant past.

"I'm going to the IGA," she said. "It's not going to be much fun for you."

The next time we got together (it was the night of that day and I picked her up at her cottage), she was again notably changed. I said to her in fact when she let me in—she took it as a joke, I suppose—that "I don't think we've met. My name is...." She was of course no one other than her elusive self. The name she gave me was Camille. I found her as before—it was her quality, various and unchanging—elusively familiar.

On our first date (we had a picnic in a misty rain, a spider web of rain), she mocked my curiosity with teasing evasions. The implication was not that her past was a secret, but that it was clear to her I already knew (without knowing I knew?) what I sought to find out. But what did I know?

I went along, played along, neither accepted nor rejected the insinuations that animated our discussion. So strong was the sense of familiarity, it embarrassed me to let out that I had forgotten the particulars of whatever past we once shared.

There were clues she threw my way. "You're not someone one forgets," she said at one point apropos of nothing.

I let myself think, Well perhaps there are people who

seem familiar whom one has never met before. If monkeys typing indiscriminately for a certain length of time can reproduce the great books, maybe genetic configurations in their complex multiplicity can also duplicate. Since no other acceptable explanation offered itself, I accepted the probability that her resemblance to Regina was circumstantial.

For the next five days, Camille and I (I thought of her sometimes as Regina II: the sequel) were virtually inseparable. I picked her up at her cottage at ten thirty each morning and returned her after dinner—sometimes after midnight—when the day had run its course. I did not ask to stay over, and no invitation was offered. We did as impulse dictated. We passed the time together as if it were dream-time. The shared assumption was we had nothing else of consequence to do but be together, no other obligations, no other places to go. On the fifth day of our accelerated acquaintance, she asked me what I thought was going on between us, and I said I didn't know and she said, sure you do.

And I said, "I'd be obliged to you if you told me what I knew."

"I can't," she said. "That would be cheating."

And then with at most ten seconds warning, it began to rain. It began to rain in torrents. We were in an open boat at the time and I took the storm as a metaphysical judgment, a kind of warning from a disinterested outsider. You are courting disaster, was the message I took away. The storm soaked me to the bone from the first blasts of rain. Lightning flashed across the ocean as I rowed frantically toward shore, Camille bailing water to no avail with a plastic cup. Waves lifted the boat onto its side, and for more than a moment it seemed almost certain that we would capsize. One of the oars slipped from its lock and floated away into the gathering dark. It was then that the boat righted itself, and I paddled us back with the remaining oar to the docking area. When we were out there, strafed by kamikaze lightning, thrashing helplessly in the storm, I thought to myself: this is it. This is the way the world ends.

I drove Camille to her cottage with barely a word exchanged between us, water dripping from our hair and eyes like unfelt tears. Then I went back to my motel to dry off. I took a hot bath and fell into bed; I had been fortunate to survive. There was no point pushing my luck any further.

I returned to my host's beach house in Provincetown the next day, my obsession with Regina redux having run its course. I can't explain my reasons—as a survivor, I suspect I felt the need to change my life—but I left East Sandwich without saying goodbye to Camille, without a word of explanation for my abrupt departure. I had run off; I had deserted my post.

My hostess, Meryll, pretended to shock at my behavior. "You're terrible," she said several times, a woman fascinated with the unacceptable.

Regina had been my most difficult wife, had caused me the most pain, had been my first love. I had no heart to go through first love a second time.

The next time I ran into her she was walking down

Commercial Street in Provincetown with an older woman. I was coming up from behind, walking with Meryll and Meryll's sister, who was up for the weekend. It would have been easy to avoid her, to slow my pace, (to cross the street), but I chose not to. Seeing her again excited me. Her Reginaness, that elusive quality that had drawn me to her, was never more apparent. She was wearing one of R's hats, a dark red, wide-brimmed thing.

She wasn't as pleased to see me, turned away when I said hello, made a point of not quite knowing who I was.

"I want to see you again," I said to her.

"What an odd thing to say," she said, showing me her back.

"Who is he?" I heard her companion ask as they walked away.

"No one," I think she said.

I didn't follow her, resisted that temptation, returned to my friends.

"She's the one, isn't she?" Meryll said. "I can see why you felt the need to run."

"Tell me," I said. "What was I running from?"

She shook a finger at me in admonishment, said, "Please!"

That night, at dinner—Meryll served lobster and french fried yams—I had no appetite, could barely sit still. I excused myself before dessert, said I wasn't feeling well, and went out for a walk.

I had no expectations. Yet at the same time I had a persuasive feeling that there was a reason beyond restiveness for what I was doing. It was a sultry night, and I found myself walking along the public pier. The sun was setting, was in the process of setting, and when you narrowed your eyes it seemed as if the entire universe was on fire. I moved to the end of the pier, offered the sunset the appropriate obeisance then turned to return. Coming toward me, only a few steps away, was the mysterious woman I had pursued and evaded, looking uncannily like an old photo of Regina that lived in my wallet for the longest time. A scarf of sunset separated us. It was as if the space between us were an unbridgeable distance. The sun rooted in my eyes.

"I'm not going to talk to you," she said, coming toward me, confronting me with her stare. "If you were any kind of gentleman, you'd go away."

When I took her at her word, spun around and walked quickly away, she called me back in outrage. "Are you being ironic with me or what?" she asked.

"I walked out in the middle of my dinner tonight to find you," I said. "If you don't want to see me, the hell with it."

"Whatever," she said, her hands on her hips, her voice rising. "You're making me crazy, you know?"

There are no transitions in this story. We are no longer on the public pier, are now having a drink at a place called The Flagship Restaurant. We are trying to remember the name of a movie starring Robert Mitchum and Kirk Douglas. When I least expect it, at a moment when we seem to have resolved all differences, Camille whispers, "Do me this favor, will you? I want you to agree that this is the last time we'll see each other. Do I have your agreement?"

I don't ask her for reasons. Arbitrariness has always

had a special fascination for me. "Whatever you say," I say.

We shake hands on a pact not to try to get in touch with each other again after this evening, our hands lingering, retaining connection. For my part, the agreement is only an excuse to touch her hand.

More bad news gradually emerges. If I hadn't run out on her in East Sandwich, she would not be going back to her former husband, a man she no longer respects. As it is, she is spending the next two days with him as a kind of trial reconciliation.

Her mood changes abruptly from ebullience to silent despair. I ask questions about her relationship with the unloved husband and get neither answers nor acknowledgement. "We have a ten percent chance of making it," she announces, making clear that the subject is closed.

That settled, we sit in the restaurant for hours talking about better times, experience a nostalgia for a shared past that, unless memory lies, never existed. Her stories lead nowhere, contradict one another, though nevertheless seem persuasively familiar and true. The unaccountable sense of familiarity reminds me of my first meeting with Mary, who was my third or fourth, in a San Francisco bar. I have the mad urge to ask Camille to marry me, though I remember there is a husband still in the picture, and I let the urge pass without acting on it.

The restaurant has to turn off their lights to get us to leave. I hear one of the waiters sigh with relief when we finally emerge from our seats. Where does the ten percent chance husband, if there really is such a figure in her life (I remain skeptical), think she is at this moment?

An uncharacteristic discretion keeps me from asking.

It is very late, and I am prepared, if reluctantly, to say goodnight, even goodbye. I lean forward to kiss her cheek. As I pull away, she suggests we go for a drive to the point to witness the sunrise.

Witness the sunrise? What an amazing request. My mouth hangs open in speechless surprise. Why extend the evening (it is almost five A.M. as it is) when we have just agreed at her mysterious urging to not see one another again.

Although I am no partisan of sunrises or fall leaves or any of the traditional mass-market esthetic diversions nature offers us in perpetual rerun, I can think of no reason to turn her down. Why not? I say, enthralled by her unexpectedness.

The next issue is whose car to take, and I suggest mine and she suggests hers, and so I say why the hell don't we take two cars, and she says, that's the kind of suggestion that ruins everything.

"Whatever you want to do," I concede. We have been walking slowly together, drifting along in the early morning mist as if we are ethereal substances ourselves when she bumps her shoulder into mine.

"Let's go in your car," she says.

We glide with our arms around each other to my car, her hand in my back pocket. When I take out my keys to open the door, she puts her arm on my shoulder and kisses me. We hold on to each other for a while—it is more affection than passion, back pressed painfully to the handle of the car door. When we get inside the car, we continue to kiss in the same affectionate nothing-at-stake manner.

We neck for awhile in the front seats, but then work our way into the back and make love (it is ghostly, like embracing a ghost) without quite undressing. I am reminded—the memory strikes me like a thorn—of a time with Regina in her father's white Buick, or was it Chevrolet, when we were both teenagers. There are other associations and some pleasures more allied with nostalgia than the moment. With the passing of the night, I have made a return trip to childhood and first love.

The sunrise wakes me. I am alone in the back of my car, my pants curled around my ankles like a serpent's embrace. What comes to mind is the conclusion of my first marriage, Regina's silent disappearance, and the extended period of disenchantment and hopelessness that followed in its wake.

Three months passed before I saw Regina redux again. I was in Toronto at the time, one of three judges for something called The North American Film Festival, which was being run by an old friend. My state of mind may be relevant here. I had not been looking for Camille, had willed her out of my thoughts after our back seat tumble in Provincetown. That's not to say that I hadn't made a small effort the morning after her disappearance, but when she proved unavailable, I consciously decided to let her slide out of my life. I thought of it as keeping the promise I had made (likely in bad faith) not to try to see her again.

I had noticed someone, an arresting-looking woman, elegantly dressed, unplaceably familiar, in the lobby of my hotel the day before we actually met. I didn't approach her.

I was at a party after one of the screenings, a last minute arrangement to showcase the female star, a six-foot teenager who as it turned out never arrived, was lingering at the bar, an eavesdropper on the forbidden (I had recently quit drinking at doctor's orders) when I felt a familiar hand on my shoulder.

"I'm overjoyed to see you again," she said, as if it were a translation from the Russian.

And I was unable—can this be believed?—to remember who she was, familiar as she seemed. "It's good to see you too," I said, trying to dredge up her name as we talked. She was not at the moment in a Regina phase, looked, if anything, more like my fourth wife, Isabelle, her reddish-brown hair in an elaborate bun.

"I thought you'd never want to see me again," she said, amused at the idea that someone might not find her irresistible, laughing to herself at her private joke. "And maybe you don't, right? Maybe you're just being polite." She kissed me in the French manner of greeting, both sides of the face given equal celebration.

I remembered the touch of her lips but not her name, remembered that she reminded me of Regina, remembered waking with my pants around my ankles, remembered that I loved her. It was only her name that eluded me.

She took my hand and looked it over, front and back, palm and knuckles. It was as if she too were searching for some identifying characteristic. For a moment, I imagined that we had each mistaken the other for someone else, someone important, irremediably lost from our lives, and that in actuality we were strangers. That fantasy lasted only for the moment of its unbidden arrival. Of course I knew her. I kissed the palm of the hand I was holding. "I'm overjoyed to see you again," I said.

"Thanks for that at least," she said. "Don't go away. I have to talk to someone, but I'll be back."

She edged through the crowd, went up to a tall bearded man, the tallest man in the room, and waited for him to lean toward her, reduce himself to her size, before she gave him a message he was not particularly happy to receive.

The man nodded, his face impassive, then reassumed his full height like an underwater swimmer rising into air. A moment later—my concentration elsewhere—she was at my side again.

"What did you say to him?" I asked.

"I said I met someone I used to know, an old old friend, and he asked me to have dinner with him. I said I wanted to talk to this friend and hoped he didn't mind."

"And what did he say?"

"You saw for yourself," she said. "He didn't say anything. He wouldn't."

"No, he wouldn't," I said. "If you broke a date with me, I wouldn't try to disguise my disappointment."

She shrugged. "It's not what you think," she said. "Before we have dinner, there's something I'd like to show you. All right? You'll have to trust me that it's important."

The appeal to trust sounded an alarm. Trusting her

was about the last thing I was prepared to do. Her name, I recalled, (why had it taken so long to come back to me?) was Camille.

Anyway, after the party, she took me to a screening of an arty independent film called *Satin Moon*, which was not an official entry in the festival.

She would not say why she wanted to me to see this film, disdained to answer the least of my questions.

"Are you in it?" I asked as the lights went out.

"You'll see," she said.

Which I did, though not perhaps as she meant it. The movie, whose title remained inexplicable (one of life's unanswered questions), was in a bleached-out color that approximated black and white, and was shown in rough cut without opening or closing titles.

The opening shot of the movie is a back view of a woman dressed all in black—not the woman herself, as it turns out, but the reflection of the woman in a full-length mirror. We are not aware of the mirror until the camera shyly draws back.

An hour of the movie has passed, and we have not seen the woman's face. The movie intends itself to be about identity, I have to believe, or the absence of identity. Other characters reveal their faces. Only the face of the woman at the center of the action remains unknown. The plot is willfully vague. The woman has committed some kind of crime in her youth and has gone unpunished. Two of her "friends" know of this crime and use their knowledge as a form of control. The nature of the crime is alluded to (someone has died), but never specified. All we know for certain is that something she has done or omitted doing, something either intended or circumstantial, has resulted in someone's death. The particulars remain frustratingly unspecific. Even more irritating is the director's continued refusal to show us the heroine's face.

When a gun presents itself, I have to believe the movie is moving toward conclusion.

The heroine abruptly turns around to confront one of her tormentors, and we see her face for the first time, though it is not her real face we see, but—it takes a moment or so to make this recognition—a lifelike mask. The small audience makes a groan of surprise at the realization. A further, perhaps private discovery is that the mask is a version of the face of the woman who has taken me to see the film. The revealed unrevealed heroine is pointing a gun at her current lover, who is one of the people who knows her guilty secret.

"Is this the way you keep people from leaving you?" he says in his brash way. "If you want my opinion, it's a poor substitute for persuasion."

"I want you out of my life, kiddo," she says.

"I'll go," he says, "but I want you to know you've got it wrong, bitch. I'm the guy who stuck by you when no one else would give you the time of day."

"It's true you're no worse than the others," she says. "The difference is, I loved you." As he turns toward the door, she shoots him, and he falls in an elaborate pirouette, blood dribbling from the corner of his mouth, his eyes open.

"Once a killer always a killer," he mutters as parting shot.

The camera meanders about the underdecorated room, looking at nothing of interest, when we hear the gun go off a second time. We see the back of the heroine, as she leaves the apartment. In long shot, we see a corpse of a woman on the floor wearing the same face-like mask as the heroine. The voice over says: "I had killed my other self."

The screen fades by degrees to black. Someone in the small audience applauds, which provokes a few more perfunctory claps. Nevertheless the film has more to say for itself. The black turns gray, reveals two, perhaps three silhouettes. There is some shadowy movement, some grappling perhaps for a gun between two or three figures, the retort of a gun, the sound of clinking glasses, a man and woman making love, a muffled scream. We see a woman in silhouette, taking off a mask. The screen fades to white, bleaches out in what seems like slow motion. We hear voices on the soundtrack, disinterested commentary like a police report or television news. The phrase "What do we really know?" insists on itself briefly. "What do we really know?"

We sat in the dark for a few more minutes, waiting for something else, some resolution perhaps, a comprehensible closure. Without warning, the houselights went on, and the shadowy images and the corresponding voices vanished into the past. I felt frustrated by the evaporation of image, as if something had been offered me (nothing I aspired to have) that had been pulled away just as I was about to take possession of it.

Camille, head down, hurried from the screening room in the wake of scattered obligatory applause. I followed her into the street a step or two behind, feeling I had just been asked to take pleasure in being mugged. "I'm sure it means something," I said, "but frankly I don't get it."

"I really didn't expect you to get it," she said. "You come to it from a completely different frame of reference. Besides, there is really nothing to get. I just wanted you to experience the film."

We were walking to the Hilton, which was the host hotel for the Festival, and I saw from the way she tilted her head when she passed on this smug consolation that she indeed had been the heroine of the movie. I felt for the first time that I was accompanying an unreasonable, possibly dangerous person.

"I'm not sure I know what you mean by different frame of reference," I said. "Is it because I'm older you think I'm someone who can't appreciate a film that uses incoherence as an esthetic principle?"

"Well," she said. "You're closed to certain things, you know. You're a man with certain attitudes about women."

"I like them," I said, "though that's not what you mean. My problem has always been that I like women too well."

"That's a self-flattering remark if I ever heard one," she said.

There was something in her tone—the inappropriate intensity of feeling—that recalled Regina at her most intolerable. "Do you want to get some dinner?" I asked. Her answer was a shrug. I followed her up to her hotel room—mine was two floors above—and said goodnight.

"Aren't you coming in?"

"I don't think so," I said. I wasn't sure what I wanted, was tired of the drift of the evening. "We'd only fight if I came in."

Her elbow jabbed me in the side. "Only people with bad consciences don't like to fight," she said.

"I thought it was the other way around," I said.

"If you stopped arguing with me," she said, "stopped being so super-rational, maybe we'd find some way of getting along."

Her hotel room was the duplicate of mine—down to the last detail—which gave me more than a moment of confusion. I couldn't wholly escape the feeling that she had usurped my space.

"Is it true you were married six times?" she asked, her accent vaguely European. She was sitting on the bed which, like mine, had an unpleasantly memorable orange cover. When I glanced around the room, I expected to see my traces and not hers.

"Does it matter?" I said. "It's the quality not the quantity that counts."

"Tell me about the first one," she said. "The first one is the only one that really matters. Did you think she was beautiful?"

"Did I think she was beautiful?" I asked myself, studying Camille's face for my answer. Regina was there for a moment, then slipped away. "She had something else," I said. "When she entered a room, no matter who else was present, all eyes turned to her."

"Yes? What does that mean?"

"She had star appeal," I said, "though she wasn't an actress. It was what caught my eye about you the first time we met, the same heartbreaking quality."

"You kind man, come sit next to me and tell me about her."

I sat down in an uncomfortable chair across from the bed and studied her astonishingly variable face. It was as if I were watching her on an out of focus television. If I could have seen her once and for all with absolute clarity, it might have made a difference in the course of my life.

Her eyes were sometimes purple, sometimes gray, sometimes a kind of blue. At times, the left seemed a different color from the right, lighter, greener.

My second wife, whose name I remembered only in flashes, had eyes that were subtly mismatched.

My third wife, as might be expected, had eyes like mine."I didn't know you were a film actress," I said. "You never mentioned it before."

"I don't think you liked that film much," she said. "You didn't like it well enough to tell me you didn't like it. Yes?"

"I liked it that well," I said, which provoked a nightlight of a smile.

It struck me that while her performance changed, or seemed to change from moment to moment, she was almost always one or another of my wives. "It took me seven years to learn how to read my first wife," I said, "and by then our marriage was beyond salvation. I still have no idea how to read you."

"To think you can read another person is a mistake," she said. As she talked, she played with her medium length brown hair, a nervous gesture that reminded me of Isabelle. "If you could read your wife, as you so oddly put it, how is it that you lost her?"

"Ambiguous text," I said. "Maybe after all it was she who lost me."

"That's not it," she said, laughing. "You're the loser. Your wife was a foreign language to you."

"Why do you think you know that?" I asked.

"I was just echoing what you were saying," she said, her mouth twisted in an ironic smile. From a cabinet in the headboard, she took out a bottle of Chivas Regal and poured us each drinks in the small plastic cups the hotel provided. "This was a gift from an admirer of my performance. I was looking for the right person to share it with."

"It's a nice thought," I said, "but I don't drink anymore."

"This is an occasion," she said. "Who knows better than you that rules have to be set aside at appropriate times."

"Why do you presume you know so much about me?"

"To us," she said, and took a drink.

"To us," I said, holding up my glass as a form of salute.

"Doesn't count if you don't drink," she said.

"Let's not get into a fight over this."

"Won't drink and he won't fight." She drained her cup and refilled it. "If you don't drink and you don't fight, what do you do?"

"I marry women I don't know what to make of," I said.

"Is that a proposal you're making? Be careful, darling, I might accept." She held out her drink to me. I took a sip.

"That's not enough," she said. "That's a child's dose."

"Why are you doing this?" I said. "What do you want from me?"

She gave me one of her slightly ironic, disapproving looks. "What do I want from him?" she asked no one. "Do I seem to want something from you? I apologize for giving the wrong impression." She yawned, turned her beautiful face away. "Did they all love you? Did you love them all?"

"Yes," I said, trying to remember. "Why does it interest you to know?"

"You thought you loved them all," she said. "There's a difference, isn't there?" She laughed at herself. "You know what I'm saying, Jack." She yawned, covering her mouth with her hand.

I took her second yawn as my cue to leave, got up from my chair, mentioned that I had to get up early the next morning to have breakfast with a distributor.

"Now that I found you again, I don't want to let you go," she said, her tone dismissive, belying her words. She held out her hand in some meaningless ritual gesture. "I think the occasion requires a kiss. Maybe I'll follow you to the ends of the earth. Does the idea frighten you? It frightens me."

I took her hand just as it seemed about to withdraw. "I don't think you mean what you say," I said. "Why should the idea of living with you frighten me? I've made mistakes before."

I was about to kiss her hand when she reclaimed it, returned it to her lap. She pouted, a self-mocking gesture. "What do I have to do to keep you from leaving?"

My disappointment in her at that moment was complete, yet I had difficulty giving her up. My back was to her when I said, "If you have trouble, as I often do, in getting through the night, why don't you come up to my room. I'm two floors above you in 707."

There was silence behind me, and I went out the door without waiting for her answer. This was my train of thought: this woman will do whatever I expect her not to do. She will not come to my room. Our moment, if there ever was one, has passed.

I didn't sleep, had a bottle of Scotch sent up, finished half of it, lost consciousness for no more than fifteen minutes at a time. The alarm clock in my head kept warning me of an unremembered appointment.

In some waking dream there was this knock on the door.

I felt for the lamp switch and knocked over the lamp, watched it float in the dark like the shadow of a bird with a snake for a tail. The rug cushioned its fall. The knocking got louder then stopped altogether. I was in a nasty mood.

"Go away," I heard myself say. I had no obligation to answer, though I was out of bed looking for pants or bathrobe to throw on, some trick to hide my nakedness in the wretched dark.

The woman awaiting me at the door was dressed in a red candy-cane shift and was, I would have sworn, Cara Lou, my fifth, a few years younger and seventy pounds lighter.

"What time is it?" she asked, a crazy question.

I had the sense that I owed her something from a long time back and that she had come from wherever to collect the debt.

"You remember, don't you?" she said shyly. "You invited me to see your hotel room. I couldn't sleep so I came by."

I stepped aside to let her pass, but she remained standing in the hallway, bars of shadow masking her face. She seemed to back away at my approach, the shadows embracing her.

"Please come in," I said.

"I'll come back another time," she said, turning to go, the room edging away from her. "I can see you didn't expect me."

"No, no, it's all right," I called after her. I was aware of the curve of her back as she walked purposefully down the long hall, the elevator ingesting her before I could find the will to follow.

I overslept the next morning, missed an appointment of potential importance with a distributor. The first thing I did on waking, however, was phone Camille's room. She was gone,the desk reported, had checked out of the hotel, at 5:30 in the morning. There was, as might have been expected, no forwarding address. She had vanished once again into the thinnest of air.

There were other stories in my life at that time—a short-lived love affair with a nun twenty years my junior, an abortive return to Hollywood as a screenwriter—but I'm going to skip six months and a week to move on with this one. I was in London on holiday, was staying in the apartment of a journalist friend, hiding out, convalescing, writing an autobiography in the form of notes to myself. No one, apart from my agent, Olympia, had cause to know I was there. I went out to dinner alone, went to the theater alone, slept alone. I had no interest in company, had moved into myself as if it were the last nuclear-free zone on earth.

One day—it was during my third week in London—I had the taunting intuition that someone was following me. I was in the Harrods food halls at the time I made the discovery. A woman dressed in black wearing a hat with a red veil—it was the third time I had run into her in the past hour—seemed to be watching me. When I moved to confront her she was gone. A ghost of bad conscience, I told myself. One needs an explanation for the inexplicable.

That same day, when I came back to my apartment after dinner, I discovered a large flat brown envelope that had been pushed under my door. The wrong door, I assumed—no one knew I was in London—but the envelope had my name on it printed in red ink in a childish hand I had seen before. I was spooked by its presence, and I put the envelope face down on an end table in my bedroom. I waited until the next morning to check out its contents.

There is something else I haven't mentioned, which I'm reluctant to mention now. Shortly after I left Toronto, I went through a bad period in which I had visions, heard and saw things no one else was hearing or seeing. I took a series of tests, but the doctors could find nothing wrong. Eventually, whatever it was seemed to heal itself.

When I first saw that envelope with my name on it on the rug just inside the door, I distrusted its reality.

The envelope was still there in the morning, face down on my desk, so I opened it. Inside was a playbill for The National Theatre production of *The School for Scan-*

dal, a curious gift. I shook out the envelope, searching for a covering letter, some tickets, some note of explanation. Finding none, I deposited the program in the waste basket, then reclaimed it. The mystery of the gift intrigued me, and I went through the program several times, looking for some hidden message. On the cast page, there was a small check mark next to the character, Lady Sneerwell. It was the only mark in the program, so I assumed (what else?) that the envelope had come from the actress playing Lady Sneerwell—her name, Caterina Page, which was not a name that meant anything to me.

Anyway, the next night, which was to be the last performance of the play—it had been running on and off in repertory for two months—I hung out at the box office waiting for the unlikely possibility of a returned ticket. The final performance had been sold out for over a week. Although I had seen two of the others in the series, for some reason I hadn't gotten around to buying a ticket for *Scandal*.

A minute or so before curtain time, an actressy young woman touched me on the shoulder and said, "Would you follow me please." She had one of those icy English voices that chilled the air.

"How do you know you have the right person?" I asked, but she seemed to know what she was doing, led me by the arm past the ticket taker, up some narrow stairs, through a door marked Private, down a long corridor, and through a second door. I found myself backstage among crew and cast and anxious silence. The curtain had just gone up, was in the process of ascent, when I was offered a seat—a wooden chair—in the wings.

It was a spectacular way to see a play, but the situation

made me uncomfortable. The actors moved by me as if I were my own hallucination. While the play was in progress, and even during the intermission, no one acknowledged my presence.

And I recognized no one. All the parts were played in masks, the production stylized in the Japanese manner. The actors depersonalized themselves, speaking their lines without inflection, which suggested something unseen going on, something immeasurably sinister behind the ritual monotony of the language.

If Lady Sneerwell was someone I knew, it seemed unlikely that she was Camille, which was what I had been prepared to believe. The actress playing Sneerwell seemed taller and somewhat heavier, though costuming might have accounted for what in any event was a theatrical illusion. And yet there were also resemblances. The malevolent Lady Sneerwell, more malevolent in this production than in others I'd seen, had a poisonous aspect that reminded me of the vengeful character Camille played in the wretched avant-garde film she had taken me to in Toronto, *Satin Moon*.

It was not Lady Sneerwell, the villainess, who presented herself to me at the play's end, but Lady Teazle, the young wife from the country, who had a comically jealous older husband. Lady Teazle had spoken the play's epilogue ("No more in vice or error to engage/ Or play the fool at large on life's great stage") and as the curtain fell, and before the others rushed out to take their calls, she pointed her finger at me.

I was waiting for her to come off stage—there were

three curtain calls—when a small man came over and said, "You can't stay here, sir. Please come along."

"I'm a guest of Lady Teazle," I said.

"Of course," he said. "Still I must remind you that Lady Teazle has changed her ways. She no longer mocks her husband's authority."

My laugh seemed to offend the man, whoever he was, small and nondescript, of no particular age. His eyes watered. One of us had missed the point. I said I understood he was only doing his job and got up from my chair to follow him out.

I am aware this section on my seventh marriage seems to be avoiding conclusion. The past has a way of prolonging itself in memory, keeping itself going through inventive elaboration. While the story is still in motion, the storyteller remains out of danger, postpones death. My "marriage" to Camille, my feckless pursuit, is both an acknowledgement of mortality and an avoidance of the final reckoning.

I waited outside the theater a few minutes, expecting Lady Teazle would join me, whoever she was, my collar up against the London night air. The moon was full, I noticed, or almost full. You could see the reflection in the Thames as if it had melted in the water like one of Dali's watches.

At some point she took my arm in the old-fashioned way, came up behind me and put her hand inside my arm as if that were its place. We were walking along Waterloo Bridge, and we stopped about midway across—that is, she stopped and I stopped with her. She was wearing a wide-brimmed purple hat, which enhanced her position as a shadowy figure. She looked amazingly like Regina.

"Why did you run out on me in Toronto?" I asked.

"I was beginning to like you too well," she said.

We went to a Chinese restaurant—a place called the Dumpling Inn—at her suggestion. I was determined this time to penetrate her various disguises.

"How did you know I was in London?" I asked during dinner."How did you manage to find me? No one, except for my agent and the friend that lent me his place, knows I'm here."

"Why should that concern you?" she said. "Isn't it enough that we're together after all this time? Possibly I saw you in the street from a distance, recognized you, and followed you home." She gave me one of Sarah Hubb's embarrassed forlorn smiles. "Possibly not."

"Which is it?"

"Does it matter? It may be that your agent is also my agent, yes? Possibly the man whose place you're staying at is a former lover. Aren't you at all glad to see me?"

"You know I am. Finding you is always a pleasure."

"So you say."

"What is it that you haven't told me?" I asked in the cab on the way to her hotel. "I think there's something I should know about you you've gone out of your way to hide."

"That's just the way it seems to you," she said. "You haven't said anything about my Lady Teazle. Did you like this performance more or less than the others?"

"I am struck by all your performances," I said.

"No," she said. "You don't really appreciate me."

I didn't argue the point, mentioned that I had focused most of my attention on Lady Sneerwell, whose name was checked in the program I received. What else was I to think?

"On some nights I play Lady Sneerwell," she said, her face tilted away. "Catarina and I have a private arrangement between us."

Although the cab stopped in front of her hotel, we didn't go inside, but went instead (a last minute change of plan) to a party for the cast of the play. A matter of diplomacy, she said. Earlier, Camille had confided that, as the only American in the cast, the other actors in the company tended to treat her with thinly disguised condescension.

"I didn't know the British used American actors in their productions," I said in the cab we took to the party.

"They do and they don't," she said with a sigh that was familiar without being immediately identifiable.

At the party she seemed as much an insider as anyone, was embraced and complimented by several members of the cast. I stood back and watched, talked only to the two people in the room I had met before, or the ones who troubled to introduce themselves.

I was lounging a few feet from the bar, observing the party as if it were a performance, when a roundfaced woman came over and asked me if I was someone she ought to have recognized. "You're the most distinguished looking man at this bash," she said. "Are you Jane's father?"

Camille, who was known as Jane to the cast, reappeared, stepped between us. "This, as a matter of fact, is my man," she said. "This is the most important man in my life." She put her arm around my waist.

The roundfaced woman and Camille talked for a moment about the theater, Camille glancing seductively at me (as Regina once had) while she made idle conversation with the actress who played Mrs. Candour. Which one was Sneerwell, I wondered aloud. She had come to the party early, Camille told me, and left before we arrived.

In the cab going to my place, Lady Teazle put her head in my lap.

"You understand I can't stay," she said as we walked up the two flights of narrow stairs to the door of my sublet, putting her arms around me from behind as I fumbled with the key. "I have to be somewhere early tomorrow." She laughed teasingly.

It was not what I anticipated. I had not been overcome this way in longer than I could remember. Once inside the door, we crushed against each other as if desire had invented us. We illustrated the principle, insisted on its primacy in human affairs. We made our bed in the living room on the faded almost colorless, oriental rug—the bedroom, some fifteen feet away, beyond our hopes.

It was curious how she seemed at once to push me away and pull me toward her.

By the early morning, we made it in to the bedroom—stumbled, crawled, arms and legs inseparably tangled, into bed. You can't eat off the floor forever.

I was too jaded, I assumed, too skeptical and world-weary, to confuse passion (or its darkened shadow) for love. I expected nothing, imagined that we would burn out in a few days and that one of us (or both) would take off, but two weeks passed and we were still together, still shaking our bones in the same bed. And—this was the oddest factor of all—Camille no longer reminded me (not much, not all the time at least) of Regina.

Almost every night when C came to bed she would announce that she was moving back into her hotel room the next day. It was like the health warning on a cigarette pack. The sex remained operatic, though impersonal, as if we were performing "passion" for an audience unused to subtlety. The word love remained whispered or unspoken, an understudy awaiting its turn.

Her nickname for me was "Daddy."

I married her in one of my dreams, a mock-marriage at some exotic carnival, our vows taken by drinking blood out of the same cup.

When we weren't making love, when love wasn't making us, Camille chewed over my life as if it were a bizarre story on the front page of *News of the World*.

"You tend to idealize women," she told me, "which has brought you nothing but misery. You think your mother was some kind of faultless saint. That's why you've been married six times. No one's good enough for a damn saint's son."

"The woman I thought was my mother was not my real mother," I said.

"Doesn't matter," she said. "By the same token, none of your wives was your real wife."

I had no idea what she meant by that.

She stayed in bed every day until noon or later, then she went out, usually to the theater, sometimes to do auditions or to shop. We fell quickly into domestic routine.

I considered hiring someone—an historian or a private detective—to investigate her past, but I never did, wanting to trust whatever untrustworthy reality she offered at the moment.

In the evenings, after a few drinks, she tended to tell stories about herself, told me once that she had been a child actress on English television.

It was hard to take anything she said at face value. "You're an American," I reminded her.

"My mother's second husband was English. We lived in Toronto for a while, then moved to London. I was nine, almost ten."

"How long did you live in London?"

"Off and on for five years. My stepfather was a barrister."

"Didn't you tell me you went to high school in California?"

"Yes." She smiled in her cryptic way.

Though at times in whispers we confessed love (at my age it is easy to confess love), we avoided talk of a future together as if the subject was too fragile to touch. I had no expectations, no view of a life with this woman beyond the next moment. We would keep going on as we were or else split up and each go on to something else. It didn't matter or it mattered too much to let it matter at all.

The moment occupied us, the unrelenting moment.

Love is a kind of addiction or prison we all struggle to escape—that was my rationale. This was my fantasy. One day, while she slept, I would slide out of bed without waking her, and go somewhere else, New York or Los Angeles or Seattle, leave without a note, with only the clothes on my back and disappear from her life. At the same time, I knew (or imagined I knew) that it was her fantasy too. The issue then was who would make the first strike, the unspeakable issue between us.

Camille remained enigmatic, though dazzlingly present, guileless and indecipherable. Could I have been wrong about her? We were getting along so well, with such apparent ease, that I began to berate myself for having a mean-spirited, distrustful nature.

I had just about set aside my plan to disappear from her life when I got a telegram from China, announcing that my journalist friend was returning to claim his apartment. Camille took the news in stride, said she knew it was only a matter of time before I would have to return to the States, that she understood that I had business matters at home that needed my attention. She was, it seemed to me, excessively understanding. I didn't suggest that she come with me; she didn't offer to come along. Neither of us suggested the alternative of other living arrangements. By a kind of mutual consent, our idyll was coming to an end.

Camille went with me in the cab to Heathrow to see me off, hugged me goodbye at the check-in counter. It was the second or third of several goodbyes. My flight went through a series of delays, its departure time pushed back forty minutes, then an hour, then two hours. We found ourselves in a tacky cocktail lounge nursing a last drink together, several last drinks. Camille had vodka over ice; I sipped beer after beer as slowly as I could, the bottles multiplying. A few years ago, a doctor had warned me to stop drinking, the consequences of going on potentially fatal.

The failure of my flight to arrive collaborated with our resistance to separation. "Don't feel you have to wait," I said. "This plane, for all we know, may never arrive."

Her face seemed to gather itself together, and I was struck again (again, again) by her uncanny resemblance to Regina. "I guess it's time for me to go, isn't it?" she said. "The idea in the theater is to get off the stage while they still want more."

"I wish you were coming with me," I said, which was not what I had been saying to myself, though became true as soon as it was spoken.

She picked up her purse from the chair at our table, lifted it in what seemed like self-mocking slow motion.

"Don't go yet," I whispered. I had a premonition that what remained ahead of me was a life alone, or with someone I was indifferent to and would grow to hate, a duration of loneliness that would test my will to survive.

Her eyes were lidded, secretive. "I'm in no rush," she said. A moment later she got up from the table, came around to my side, stood behind me, touched my cheek with her palm. "I have to go," she said under her breath. "You understand?"

I nodded in concurrence. "Of course." I felt like someone in a movie who had been shot in the heart and refused to fall.

"Do you think a few minutes more will make a difference?" she said.

I threw some money on the table, gave her one last hug (the longest, the last of lasts) and walked away. It was time to go home.

Who was she anyway?

"I'll get in touch when I come back to the States," she called to me.

Waiting at the boarding gate for my plane, reading a "Time Out" to pass the time (the flight was now a full two hours late), I had another change of heart. I left the airport without collecting my bags (they could fly back to New York without me) and queued up for a taxi. The wait was short. I was inspired, took the taxi to the Regency and went directly to Camille's room without announcing myself by phone.

When she opened the door, looking ill with surprise, looking back at me like a mirror image, I said, "I couldn't leave without you. I want you to come with me." It was then that I sensed, something in her manner, something in the way she was standing, that there was someone in the room with her.

She said, without blinking, without a moment's apparent doubt, "I can't. Sorry."

"I should have said something earlier, but sometimes the things we mean have difficulty getting said." I said. "We could get married in New York. I want to spend the rest of my life with you."

She seemed to smile, offering me a momentary illusion of hope and with it an attendant anxiety. "It's not possible," she said. "It's just not possible."

I didn't argue my case, took the elevator down to the empty lobby and sat for a while in a deceptively uncomfortable chair, musing on nothing. I suffered the anxious exhilaration one feels, having escaped a nearly fatal disaster. Had the chair been at all accommodating, I would have given myself to it. My motor was running too fast to allow for sleep. As it was, I nodded off from time to time, imagined myself rising from my uncomfortable chair and going somewhere—the airport, another hotel,

Los Angeles—as if I had converted to spirit and was severing ties with my earthworn body.

I also imagined that Camille would abruptly appear to announce that she had thought it over and changed her mind. Or that—I had missed the point—no, when you broke the code, meant: of course darling, yes, yes.

Having played out the major scenarios between us in my imagination, I hurried back to Heathrow, got a seat on the 8:20 Concorde and returned to New York, spirit and body intact, virtually before I left London.

There was a telegram waiting for me at the door to my apartment. "Disregard first answer," it read. "More to follow."

I telegraphed back, a message I regretted five minutes after it was gone: "Some refusals are irrevocable." My first impulse had always been to do the wrong thing. My second was to rationalize it away.

Her message to follow, which may have been sent before she received mine, read in its entirety: "Whether We Marry Or Not, I Am Already Yours." It was signed Lady Teazle.

I pretended to myself not to know what she meant, let a month pass before phoning her. She was not at the same hotel, nor was she still associated with the same theater group. No one seemed to know precisely where she had gone. Berlin, someone had heard. To make a movie with Werner Herzog. Someone else said she was doing an opera in Japan. A third source said she had come to New York.

I like to believe she is in New York. Intuition tells me that she is living near me, on the same street or even in the same building, without letting her presence be known. It's not impossible that I've passed her in the street without recognition. Who is she really? She is an actress with an invented past who has some mysterious connection to my life. The woman is a virtual chameleon, can appear to be whoever it amuses her to be. She might be Regina's daughter from another marriage. Or Regina herself frozen in time. Or.... The question of who she is and how she knows so much about my past may never be answered. Or perhaps it has been answered, and I've willfully missed the point. Whoever she is, she is, as she says, mine. I see her reflection everywhere, in the mind's eye, in the various mirrors of my apartment, in hallucinations and dreams. She is persistently present. She is inescapable.

8
In the Arms of Ghosts

He was about to unmask a murderer, had his hand on the lower portion of the mask, when the doorbell sent a shock wave through his system.

Suddenly he was on his feet, gun in hand, approaching the door. The door also approached him, had its own separate agenda. "Yes?" he heard himself ask.

"I have to talk to you," a woman's voice said.

He pointed the gun to the right of the door, regretted the burden of having to aim at something. "It's the middle of the fucking night. Come back tomorrow."

"It's important that I talk to you now," she said.

He unlatched the door and stepped to the side, to

behind the door.

"It's open," he said.

For what seemed like several minutes, though was probably only seconds, there was not even a heartbeat on the other side of the doorway. It was a silence enhanced to a kind of unbearable non-pitch.

The living room light flickered behind his ear, and he turned his head to see what was amiss. When he turned back, the door was already open and a largish shadow was moving toward him in a menacing way.

He held the gun out in front of him, thrust it at the life-size shadow, which he would have sworn was coming toward him. "Go away," he said. "I have a gun."

Did it listen to him? No, it didn't.

He took a defensive posture, fired a warning shot, intending only to frighten and dissuade. The art deco standing lamp with the glass shade went over, sparks flying from the outlet as it tore itself from the wall. There was another crash, the second making common cause with the first. The shadow stalking him also tumbled.

There was an afterimage perhaps illuminated from the sparks coming out of the wall. He knew, without actually seeing her, that the woman who had come through his door was Cara Lou, his fifth wife. When he got the light on, she was sleeping in a bed of shattered glass.

He felt for her pulse, put his ear against her heart. There were distant murmurs like trapped voices. That was a hopeful sign. Also, he could find no wound. His own breathing was so loud it made it difficult to tune in to hers. It was virtually impossible, he told himself, improbable if not impossible, to hear both of them breathe at the same time. Looking the other way, brushing the diamonds of glass from his pants, he noticed out of the corner of his eye what appeared to be a scarlet circular mark on her temple abutting the hair line. The longer he studied the mark, which gave off a kind of glow, the more pronounced it seemed. When he got closer he could see that it might be a wound—it stared like a tiny doll's eye—but it seemed too small to have been made by a bullet.

He woke slumped in a chair, lamplight directly in his face. The body had been removed, the room restored to its former pristine elegance. Some might say it had been a dream, but he tended to believe that he never slept. And how could you be haunted by dreams if you never slept? When he was younger he could pass off the inexplicable with irony. He had reached a point in his life where he took all his experiences, no matter how far out, no matter that they defied his secret belief in the reasonableness of the universe, with absolute seriousness.

He'd been trying to write the story of his seven marriages in a way that would permit him to recapture his life, to give it the esthetic form it lacked in real time. His adult experience had from the start mocked his faith in the rational. What he wanted was a satisfying closure. He was desperate to make sense—any kind of sense—of a life that had avoided the sensible at all costs.

He rewrites the first sentence again and again, has difficulty accommodating himself to the imprecision of language. At the end of the first week, he has written two surviving pages. Although accurate in its way, with only minor distortions for the sake of emphasis, it reads, much of it, most of it, like lies.

At that point, our mutual agent, Olympia, puts him in touch with me. I am first of all a novelist, but I've done some anonymous collaborating now and then with people who have difficulty telling their own stories. My name is Joshua Quartz.

After an extended period of negotiation, he hires me to help him complete his story.

In our first conversation, he insists he is not interested in my participation, but after a frustrating period of miniscule progress, he calls me back to solicit my help. "Time is slipping away," he tells me. "It concerns me that I'm not going to be around long enough to finish what I've started."

"I'm into a new novel," I say. "I don't really have time to take this on."

"I'll pay you for your time at whatever rate you think is fair," he says.

"What I'm doing means more to me than money," I say. "I'll need some time to think it over."

He is impatient, apparently desperate. "You're the man I want, Josh," he says, "but I don't have time to fool around. I might be dead tomorrow. You'll have to give me your answer in the next ten minutes."

"Why don't I come over, and we'll talk face to face."

"That's not the way I do business, Josh," he says. "I don't go face to face with anyone any more. Give me your address, and I'll send you my notes."

We had spoken several times on the phone and had exchanged two sets of letters before he would allow me to come to his east side apartment for a visit. Trust was not his strong suit. The notes he had sent me, which were in four thick spiral notebooks, were full of gaps and unanswerable questions. But that alone wasn't the reason I felt compelled to see him. If I was going to collaborate with him on his biography, I wanted to see for myself—face to face—the most recent face of my collaborator.

Olympia had repeatedly warned me that he could be irascible (he was thought by some to be wholly unreasonable, maybe even mad), and I was on my guard when I knocked on his door one cool March morning.

For what seemed like almost five minutes there was no answer, though he had agreed to my visit and must have been expecting me. "No one home," a voice barked from just behind the closed door. "Get lost."

"I'm afraid I'm a few minutes early," I said. "It's Josh Quartz. We have an appointment for ten."

The door opened in a kind of slow motion, and I stepped in, expecting to be greeted by my host. But no one was there, which gave me a turn, which must have left my mouth hanging somewhat ajar. In the next moment, a shadowy figure darted out from behind the door, a gun in his hand pointed toward my left ear.

"Hey, wait a minute," I said. "No need for that."

He seemed surprised that I was afraid of the gun in his hand (surprised perhaps that it was even there), and he slipped it into his belt. "Don't concern yourself, Josh," he said. "I've gotten into the habit of taking no chances. It's a sad commentary on the times."

The vestibule was unlit and my first sense of him was of a kind of bear on stilts. He stood back, signalling me to precede him into the living room, which was a handsome large room, immaculate on one side and cluttered with books and debris on the other. I sat on a gold velvet couch at his invitation while he stood across from me and paced. He was well over six feet and slightly stooped, had a wreath of fierce white hair on his shiny bald head, and a reddish-gray beard of almost a week's growth. His face was almost perfectly round and seemed untouched by experience as if its age lines had been effaced. While the rest of him had aged accordingly (I estimated his age from the documents he had given me at sixty-one), his face remained a child's.

"Am I what you expected?" he asked, barking his question at me.

"No," I said, pinned by the directness of the question, unable to lie. "Not exactly." I expected him to ask what my expectation had been or what the disparity was, but he didn't, merely grunted his acknowledgement.

"I don't know how to entertain visitors any more," he said with a groan. "I've fallen out of the habit, Josh." He moved his mouth as if he were trying without success to smile or chewing on the memory of a former meal. "To be fair about this, you invited yourself here. So you have no choice, do you, but to make the best of the nothing you get." He broke into a spasmodic laugh as if responding despite himself to someone else's joke.

"I'll try not to take up too much of your time, sir," I

said. “I have a few questions, mostly matters of clarification.”

He barked a three syllable laugh. “Josh, you can take up my time or you can put it down,” he whispered hoarsely. “At the moment, you’re sole heir to all the time I’ve got.”

He pointed his finger at my chest as if it were the gun.

I had some questions jotted down on a sheet of paper, which I took out from my inside jacket pocket. His fierce towering pacing presence made it hard to begin. I read through my list, painfully aware of the triviality or inappropriateness of what had seemed, when I put them down, useful inquiries. I started with, “Which of your seven wives would you say was your favorite?”

“You can do better than that, Josh, can’t you?” he barked, stopping his pacing just long enough to censure me with a stare. “That’s not a real question, author. When anyone asks me that question, I always say the last one. I don’t know if it’s true—what’s true, for God’s sake?—but it’s the answer I like to give.” He troubled his mouth into a half-smile.

“You’ve indicated on the phone that you believe your former wives and maybe some other women as well are in some kind of malicious conspiracy against you. Do you...”

“That’s only a supposition,” he interrupted. “A possible explanation for a perceived threat.”

“I get that,” I said. “In this possible conspiracy, which of your wives would you say was the most potentially dangerous? Who’s at the center of the plot?”

“The last one,” he said, pursing his lips. “Same answer, different question.”

“By the last one, you mean Camille. Is that right?”

"Whatever I say, I mean," he said, waving off my question with a world-weary gesture. I read out another question from my list. "Have you remained in touch with any of your wives and, if so, which ones?"

"None," he shouted, "never. Not for years. Sarah,who is in Los Angeles and has done some directing, sends me a card on my birthday without fail. Sometimes we talk on the phone, but not to my knowledge in the last three or four years. Okay? Isabelle had a brief run as an actress in porno films—I used to rent her latest from Screen Dreams as a way of keeping in touch. I wrote to her a few times to tell her I thought she was demeaning her talent, but I never got an answer. I dream of Cara Lou. I get boxes of poisoned candy from Lulu. I see Camille everywhere."

"In respect to Isabelle: she spoke no English—how could she have auditioned with you for a part in a movie? Do you recall the incident I'm talking about?"

"I forget nothing," he said. "The part she auditioned for was that of a French woman who spoke no English. Whatever English words the part required she memorized and mispronounced. She had a feral quality that was quite unique."

"In respect to Cara Lou: when she asked you to marry her, she told you she had no more than five years to live. There's no indication in your notes as to what happened to her. In some places, you refer to her as if she were still alive. Did she lie to you about her illness? That needs clarification."

"I don't like to call anybody a liar," he said, "but isn't everyone. Cara Lou, she was something of a hypochondriac. She may have believed she was dying. How do I know what she believed? Sometimes she calls without speaking. There's some devil in all that flesh. Do I know she's alive? I know nothing about it. But if you ask me if she's alive, I'll swear to you she is." He looked off into the distance, sighed, and turned silent. "I don't sleep. I never sleep." He closed his eyes for an instant, faded. "This is not sleeping," he mumbled, the hollow voice like an echo.

"I'll come back another time," I said.

His eyes snapped open, stared at me with obvious displeasure. "Do you think I'm a fool?" he asked in a whisper. Then he raised his voice, "Who the fuck do you think you are to come into my house and humor me? If you have any more questions, ask them. If you don't, waltz out the door, Matilda."

I was taken aback by the abrupt change in his demeanor, took occasion to glance at my notes in order to regain composure. When I looked back at him, I caught him in a sly half-smile. "There's no mention of children in your account," I said."Were there any children, apart from the possibility of Camille, and if there were, are you in touch with any of them?"

He moaned as if in pain. "What did I say before when you asked me that?" he said.

"I didn't ask that question before," I said.

He turned his back to me and walked ceremoniously out of the room. Was this another one of his games? I waited ten minutes, then got up to leave. "I'm going," I called to him. There was no request for my return.

It is a Friday in early April, a residue of blackish snow along the curb, when a tall stooped man in a lightweight suede jacket ventures outside for the first time in several months. He has two weeks' growth of reddish-gray beard, which serves him as a disguise. As he walks from Park Avenue across Madison to Fifth, he loses track of time and distance.

He refuses to acknowledge that someone is following him, though he is aware that much of the evidence points in that direction.

The sun goes goes behind clouds as he crosses Fifth Avenue, and he is abruptly aware that it is colder than he had cause to expect. He is going nowhere, as he sees it, just walking around, waiting for a destination to take him in hand. The park, toward which he'd been heading, is not where he wants to find himself, so he makes a choice to go the other way, to go east, which will take him to the river. He likes the idea of visiting an open space. He is weary of secret places, is tired to death of hiding out.

He passes a pet shop on Third Avenue and goes inside, hires (buys with an agreement to return in two days for full refund if not absolutely satisfied) a large dog (three-quarters Shepherd, one-quarter unthinkable mix) for protection. The pimply-faced clerk says the dog is loyal to a fault and will bond with a new owner as soon as he accepts his authority. The dog snarls at him as he leads him from the store on his training leash.

The creature's name, according to the clerk, is King. "I'm going to make you a star, King," he whispers to the dog as they begin their walk together to the river. "You're going to be the sensation of a nation, fella, a role model for the lesser of the species. Just for God's sake don't tug on the leash. It's not companionable, pal. And don't, if you want to retain my undying affection, step on my feet." He realizes when the dog squats to take a leak that King is a she, a bitch so to speak. Another example of gender confusion. Why not?

When they arrive at the line-up of benches facing the river, he can't imagine why he chose to go there. If he doesn't take notes on what he does he loses the intention before it is completed. His memory is a well, filled with undrinkable water.

He sits down on a bench with an unobstructed view, and waits for his pursuer to reveal herself. King, who has apparently come to terms with his new relationship, lies uncomplainingly at his feet.

A woman he doesn't know, doesn't think he knows, an arty type with glasses, in her late thirties, establishes herself on the bench directly to his right. She reads or pretends to read a hardback book, which she holds in front of her face when he glances at her. The title, which he thinks he is meant to read, is *The Secret Woman.* He orders King to "stay" and moves over to the woman's bench without waiting for a direct invitation.

"It takes some doing to get your attention," she says, her head turned away as if she were talking to some invisible presence on the other side.

The sun slides behind clouds and the wind surges off the water. He embraces himself to keep warm.

"You live alone," she says. "Don't you? I know the signs. You have no one to look after you. I think that's sad. Still, you're not my problem."

"I don't need anyone to look after me," he says, blowing on his hands. "It's not my fault the sun ran for cover."

The dog snarls at something in his dream, then whines piteously.

"That dog will do anything for me," he says. "We've been bonded."

"The fact is, you're not appropriately dressed, are you?" she says. "You use need as a form of seduction. Your helplessness is what makes you so attractive to women."

He sits on his hands to warm them. "You're not Camille, doing one of your numbers, are you? No, I can see you're not Camille. What do you want from me?"

"My name is Rosetta," she says. "Look, I live a few blocks from here. I can lend you something to wear—my former husband, not otherwise generous, left a closet full of clothes behind."

Her kindness aggravates his suspicion, but he gets up to go with her nevertheless. He has come this far. After two disconcerting turns—a right followed by a left—he remembers that he has forgotten King. Turning his head, he discovers the dog is following him, the leash slapping along the sidewalk. "This is it," she says just at the point when he is too tired to go any further.

It is a new building with a fountain in front, glitzy, though without style. Her apartment is on the third floor and as he waits for her to unlock the door she says, "I hardly live here. My real home is somewhere else."

"What do I do with the dog?"

"Is that dog really yours? I don't know what to say. I'd rather not have it in the apartment."

The apartment is unfurnished except for a hooded standing lamp with an orange stem and two matching under-upholstered green chairs facing each other.

"Have a seat," she says. "This won't take long."

He thinks to ask her if she's a therapist—the facing chairs—but he walks around instead looking at the travel posters on the walls while she goes into the other of her two rooms.

The outside view the room offers is of the back of a building similar to his own. The more he studies the look-alike building, the surer he becomes that he is actually just around the corner from where he lives. The proximity gives him a sense of security, which he immediately distrusts.

Although her apartment is overheated, he is unable to get warm. He rubs his hands together to restore circulation, but they remain mostly numb. The cold seems to own them. What's taking the woman so long?

He hears murmuring sounds coming from the next room, which aggravates a suspicious nature. What's going on? Is there someone else in the apartment beside the woman? Has he been set up? The woman has been gone far too long. He considers his options, considers opening the outside door and introducing the element of the dog into the equation, considers leaving (escaping to home), before she returns. His panic embarrasses him. His priority, in any crisis, is to discover how things turn out. If he runs away to escape possible danger, he will never know what danger it was he ran away to escape.

When she reappears, she holds out her empty hands in front of her. He has the impression that she is offering him something that he is not privileged to see. "The last time I was here," she says, "the closet was overrunning with his clothes. I'm sorry. He must have come back and taken them when I wasn't around."

"That's all right," he says. "It's easy for me to get home from here." He makes it a point not to tell her where he lives. When he rubs his hands together they feel like strangers.

"I feel so stupid bringing you here for nothing," she says. "Is there anything I can do to make it up to you?"

He looks at her, studies her face, to see what she's really saying. Her glasses, which are tinted, provide her with a kind of disguise.

Instinct warns him that he ought to leave—there was the dog to return or keep (what had he done with King?)—but she is appealing, and he has not had a woman since his break up with Camille.

King, who waits for him in the hall, scratches at the door from time to time to make her presence felt.

He slips out, goes around the corner to his apartment, finds that his key no longer opens his door, finds that a woman with his own initials has been living in his place in his absence, finds that there is no one in the building (no one who is at home) who remembers him. He accepts the impossible situation with only minor resistance. Isn't this what was bound to happen? His mistake was to leave his penthouse apartment in the first place. When he finds himself out on the street with nowhere to go, he retraces his steps.

His luck holds. Rosetta invites him in, says she is glad to have him back, embracing him when he steps through the door. He is shivering from the cold. This woman is strange, he remarks to himself, after she leads him by the hand into the bedroom. It is not a new perception, the strangeness of the woman. It is her oddness that makes it possible for him to trust her. No one wanting to deceive would pretend to be such an unlikely person.

"Is there something special you would like?" she asks as if she were the hostess of a sexual concession. She removes her blouse and hangs it on the back of a chair. She wears no bra. Her breasts are modest and perhaps elegant. He removes the suede jacket he is wearing (a gift from Sara Hubb), sheds it like snake skin, tossing it inaccurately in the direction of the room's one chair. He is still fully dressed, though he feels uncovered, his secrets (which are none, which are nothing) given away. His secrets fly about the room.

"Take your pants off," she says, no stranger to authority. She is in the process of sliding out of her black-striped gray jeans, which had seemed painted on.

They have not yet touched. Is it excitement? He has difficulty catching his breath, holds his hand to his heart.

He removes his pants with more than usual reluctance. She is two or three steps ahead, wears only glasses and black (perhaps silk) panties (an elegant purple flower at center stage), her face without identifiable expression. She releases her light brown hair, which had been in a bun, and he watches it fall with a sigh of admiration.

No matter how many women you've had, the shyness is always there the first time. Or perhaps as you get older, you get increasingly reluctant about showing yourself without the ready-made dignity of costume. His stomach protrudes from under his shirt, asserts itself.

"Would you like to lie down?" she asks.

He leans forward and kisses her left breast, which is sadder than the other, more in need of admiration.

"Most men prefer that one," she says.

Has he made the wrong choice again? There is always chance for restitution. He brushes the nipple of the unpreferred breast with the tip of his tongue.

"I feel shy with you," she says. "Would it be all right if we talked a little more?"

"You're a beautiful woman," he says.

"No," she says. "Thank you, but I mean talk about yourself. Ordinary things—the kind of details that make a life. Wives, children, things you wanted to do and never did. Have you ever been married?"

The question seems inescapable. "I've never been married," he says. "That's the answer I give when anyone asks if I've ever been married."

"Uhh," she says, one of those ambiguous moans. "I'm a one-time loser myself. I never knew where he was coming from." Moving into the bed, under the white comforter dotted with small black flowers.

He assumes that that concludes their talk, this phase of it. As he moves into her queen-sized bed, he feels an overwhelming desire to confess something. I'm unworthy of you, he wants to say. Instead, he whispers, "May I have this dance, sweetheart?" It is only a joke or a passing remark disguised as a joke. Her answer is not worth repeating. She may have said nothing at all.

He hears what sounds like someone dancing in the closet among empty hangers and old shoes. It may be only the wind, which seems to rub itself against the window.

"My name is Rosetta," she whispers to him. "Like the stone. When you make love to me, I'd like it if you'd say my name."

"Rosetta."

"Yes. I like that. You're my sweetheart."

She is on top, rides him like a seesaw. He says her name, holds it between his teeth.

"What do you like?" she asks.

"I like everything about you, Rosetta," he says. "If it's all the same to you, I prefer to be the one on top." They turn around as if they've done this trick before.

"You're good," she says. "You know that, right? Yes? Silly me. Not to rush, sweetheart. We have the afternoon ahead of us. And the evening. And the next day. Keep going. Yes. Your wives must have been crazy to let you get away. Say my name, darling."

"Rosetta...I have a confession to make." He has difficulty catching his breath, is unable to continue. What's the story?

"You're my guy," she says. "Don't stop. Oh, faster, yes."

He has found his rhythm, is moving so fast it's like not moving. Can he keep it up, that's the question, can he keep going, can he rise and fall like a summer day and for how much longer? Can he keep it going for another hour? If you refuse to stop, there's always the possibility that you can go on indefinitely, he tells himself. Who's to say no? "Rosetta," he remembers to say, tasting the name as he gives it back to her. They say the first love is so indelible, the ones that follow exist in the heart like shadows of the original. For him the photo in the heart's album has always been the last.

"I'd like to be on top now," she says, "if it's no trouble. I tend to get antsy if I don't know what's going to happen next."

A turnabout is effected with the least possible effort. They are a team, seem to have practiced together for years, which we know to be illusion. She moves away, seeks the air and returns, as if keeping time to secret music. On his back, he can see beyond her to the barely visible cupids carved into the ceiling.

"Say my name," she demands.

He has trouble remembering who she is. "Regina."

She pushes against his chest and rises into the air, holds herself above him, her shadow across his face. Her return to earth is never without surprise.

"I would have picked you out of a crowd," she says.

He is grateful for the compliment. While making love, he recites his wives' names to himself—a litany of lost loves. They are all there, seated in order of appearance around the mind's table. Her name is the last to find his tongue. "Rosetta."

"That's right, my darling. Say it."

As soon as he comes—the moment after—the moment after the moment after (he had hoped to go on forever, for God's sake), the bedstead lamp blinks out. It is like a flash of memory: he glimpses heartbreak. A menacing shadow pours from the closet. Has someone been there all this time? What's going on? For a moment almost all his wives are in the room, standing at the foot of the bed in a semi-circle. They are smiling, but it is not in his view a sympathetic smile. It is the kind of smile you would run a mile in a snow storm in bare feet to avoid.

What's the story? he asks himself. A shadow slides

along the wall, comes down on top of him like a reckoning, its hand over his mouth. "I have you now," a woman's voice says. It is either Regina or Camille. The others congregate, make idle conversation. He notices Sarah Hubb and a thinned down Cara Lou, and one who may or may not be Lulu. Lulu, if that's who it is, is virtually unrecognizable. The two other women in the room are imposters—one of them resembles the faded Nadia.

"I've had enough of your demands," he says to the crowd. "I want to live out my remaining days with some portion of kindness and passion." No one points out to him the potential contradiction inherent in his request.

Some of the women get into the huge bed with him, some sit in chairs on the sidelines. This is what marriage comes to, he tells himself. And what he gets are variations on the same metaphysical questions. Who's on top? Who's on bottom? Is he getting fucked or what? Is it love to get fucked? Is it fun? Is that all there is? Rosetta is holding his own gun to his head. Which is pushy and suggests distrust. He pushes the gun aside with the back of his hand. This is taking things too far he tells her. All at once is not the game plan at this late date, an idle unimaginable aspiration. Still, they won't go away for the asking. Someone's hand fits over his mouth. One (Regina or Isabelle) under him, one on top (Lulu, damn her!) one on each side (the fucking imposters here). They worry him with passion; they torture him with kindness. Enough, he says. Stop already. He doesn't believe it is happening, yet he is unable to will himself elsewhere. When you've been everywhere, where else is there to go? There are too many wives in the bed and not enough hands (or fingers on hands) or balls or pricks or mouths or noses or toes to keep everyone happy. Whose dance is this anyway? When he puts his tongue between the first woman's legs, the others complain of social inequities. What do you think you're doing? they say. That one has had her turn. The same feckless theme: your dance or mine? Queried as to preference, he is cautious with his answer, says he loves them all, loves them like the first light of morning, like a cool drink of water in the night, like love itself. That's not the answer anyone wants to hear. That's no answer at all. Words, don't fail me now, he says to himself. Words, do your stuff. He makes his excuses to each wife in turn. It is the same excuse. He felt, no matter who he was with, no matter how good it was in itself, that there was something else out there that he was missing. He has no regrets. He regrets everything.

What's it all about? Just when he's finally got it right, got it down to an exact science, the game is all but over. Like this. Mouth on wife one, prick in wife seven, right hand in wife two, left in wife five, a big toe on each foot for the fucking imposters. What's the story? This can't be love, can it? Can it? This is the story of his life. This is the rough cut of the movie of the story of his life. It can't be love, can it, when you're having more than one? Who says? This is life-threatening pleasure, folks. This is sucking and fucking, ladies and genitals. This is the final fucking dream. This is in and out, up and down, keep the motor running, this is the unredeemable redeemed, this is I'd rather be good than lucky time. So why can't this be love? This is sex as death, that's why. This is love on ice, sucker. This is the final futile show. Your heartbreak or mine? The same unanswerable questions. And he's the name before the title, has finally made it to the top. This is the movie of the play adapted from the novel based loosely on an incident in his past it pleased him to forget. It all comes to the same thing. This is closing night after all. This is the last act. Why not call it love? What do you say? Who's going to know the difference? Who's even going to remember what you called it? In the last act, he gets to have them one at a time and in a manner of fucking all at once. It's never been so good. This is the life that almost was. What's going on, sweetheart? Is this the best dream of all, or what? They all love him in this dream. Can you believe it? They all love to love him, and he loves to be loved by them. But hey, who's on top? That doesn't matter in the long run. We're talking love here, major passion. Each man a king in his own head—that's the final dream. In and out, up and down—old times. What else is new? How long can he last? As far as love's wings take him. We're talking the triumph of feeling over cynical indifference. It's love, right? It's been his lifelong ambition to discover a cure for heartlessness (you got to try it on yourself first) and to make love forever. Who says he can't? Who says...? Who....